bones picked clean

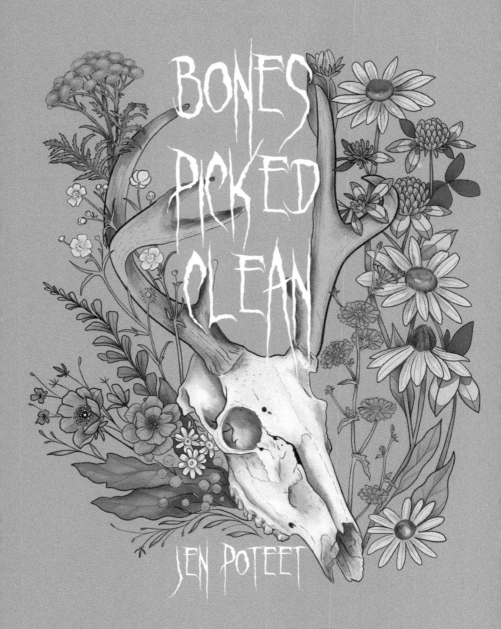

BONES PICKED CLEAN

JEN POTEET

Bones Picked Clean
by Jen Poteet

Cover Design by Jen Poteet

Interior design by Suzanne Shelden
Shelden Studios
Prince Frederick, Maryland
sheldenstudios@comcast.net

A note on type: cover and section heads are set in Ghastly Panic;
headers and poetry in Ghost Town Condensed;
paragraph text is set in Garamond Premier Pro

Library of Congress
Cataloging-in-Publication Data

ISBN: 978-1-960522-07-8

Printed in the United States of America
First Edition

Dedication

This book is for anyone who has ever been asked,

"why can't you be like everyone else?"

This book is for folks like me.

This book is for the Black Sheep.

Table of Contents

Part One

Chapter 1 Root, Hog or Die   3
Chapter 2 Home is where the Holler is   8
Chapter 3 Superstitions, Haints and Heebie-Jeebies   12
Chapter 4 Pretty Is as Pretty Does   17
Chapter 5 By the Skin of Their Teeth   22
Chapter 6 Fit to be Tied   26
Chapter 7 That Dog Won't Hunt   31
Chapter 8 Be Careful What you Wish For   35
Chapter 9 Hotter than a Sinner in Church   42
Chapter 10 There's a Fox in the Henhouse   47
Chapter 11 The Knocking   51

Part Two

Chapter 12 As I Live and Breathe   58
Chapter 13 Beggars Can't Be Choosers   63
Chapter 14 A Bird in the Hand is Worth Two in the Bush   67
Chapter 15 Where There's Bees There's Honey   71
Chapter 16 What Can't be Cured Must be Endured   78
Chapter 17 You Can't Make a Silk Purse out of a Sow's Ear   80
Chapter 18 Fair to Middlin'   88
Chapter 19 Put your Money Where Your Mouth Is   98
Chapter 20 Can't See the Forest for the Trees   104

Part Three

Chapter 21 Lord Willing and the Creek Don't Rise   114
Chapter 22 Don't Count your Chickens Before they Hatch   118
Chapter 23 Out of the Frying Pan and Into the Fire   126
Chapter 24 Pot Calling the Kettle Black   130
Chapter 25 Shit or Get Off the Pot   136
Chapter 26 What Goes Around Comes Around   142
Epilogue   147
Giving Credit Where Credit's Due   149
About the Author   153

Follow me into the forest.

                         Step into the trees.
Leave behind the hustle and bustle of life.

         Here you will find the solace you seek.
         The canopy above your head rustles in the soft breeze.
Birdsong and insect calls serenade you as you walk.
         Your footsteps land on leaves damp with weather.
         Each step releases the cloying scent
                              of their rot thickly upon the air.

         Distractions are long gone, but wonders abound.
                  The earthen floor writhes with living things.
         Things that crawl in

                                   and out
      of a nearby carcass.

         Kind of gross but we're in nature.

         Wildlife flits around.
         You catch a glimpse out of the corner of your eye
         but when you turn your face there's nothing there.
         Look, mushrooms grow from a fallen branch.
         A brook babbles, sparkling under beams of sunlight.
         So tranquil
                           and yet

Left with nothing but the thoughts in your head,
            it becomes too much.
    Sick of the solitude you start to whistle.
    A clever bird repeats the tune.
    Tickled pink you whistle again.
    Only this time, it sounds odd.

    Again! That shadow just out of sight.
    Is it silent?
    Every other noise has stopped
                as if the woods itself is holding its breath.
    An overwhelming feeling of dread settles into your bones.

Your heartbeat thunders in your ears.

    Ba-Boom.

                Ba-Boom.

    The hair on your arms stand on end and your flesh pebbles.
    Sweat drips in rivulets down your back
                even though you are freezing.
    A twig snaps, you swing toward the noise.

    You are not alone.

PART ONE

CHAPTER 1
ROOT, HOG OR DIE

Do you ever just stop and marvel at being alive? Or look at the person next to you and think how wonderful it is that you're alive at the same time? As the years go on, we'll collect other people and experiences that mold and shape us. Each time it happens we become a different version of ourselves. Yet the ghosts of our pasts will always haunt us. And what about death? It can leave a black mark on our soul, or it can start a new beginning.

Our story starts with a death.

Chicory Lynn did not remember much about her momma except there was a little hole where her front teeth met that was shaped like a diamond. This hole was from the pipe she often used. Granny was teaching Chicory shapes and she was proud to know what a diamond shape was. She knew her colors and how to write her name too.

When Chicory's momma would talk, that hole would turn her words to whistles and it would get her laughing so hard. The down deep whole belly kind of laughing. That's about all she remembers.

But Chicory's momma was always gone. So the *gone for good that is dead* didn't really register, because how can you miss someone who ain't ever there? Even when her momma was sitting in the same room she'd been somewhere else in her mind.

On the day of her momma's funeral, all Chicory could do was wait impatiently for the service to be over. All those strangers whispering sounded like wind blowing through tall grass. It made Chicory wish to be outside. Instead, she was sneezing from the too sweet smell of lilies. She had to stand in the too small shoes Gran had gotten at the Goodwill. They pinched her pinky toes, but all the same, the patent leather pair had little bows on top, and Chic felt princess pretty in them and her new dress. She was too young to understand the pity in the eyes of all those big people when they gazed at her. She was also too young to know what it meant to be an orphan.

She sat next to her Gran all the way up in the front row. Gran had put on her best dress and the preacher called her Ms. Winifred Goodwin, even though she was known as Granny to all. They sat and listened to the sermon the preacher had prepared. Gran had said the man was always around for marrying or burying. While she listened to his deep voice, she could not comprehend the words that were spoken. Gran explained, "It's Psalms something. It's always Psalms something."

Winifred Goodwin's only child was lying in a pine box. Her heart was splitting in two, her feelings all mixed up. The pain of seeing her beautiful daughter's body, disfigured from its battle with drugs, was sharp. Sharper still was guilt. Guilt from wondering where she went wrong mothering. Guilt from the staggering relief her daughter was at peace.

Gran had done nothing but worry herself sick for the past decade and her body sure felt older. She wasn't a spring chicken. She had her daughter later in life and now she would have to live long enough to raise her grandchild. That task she wouldn't mind, Chicory was an easy child. A pale and tiny thing that was always keeping quiet. Even in the first few days of her coming to live with Gran, nothing but skin and bones toddling around, she rarely cried. Gran had hoped the baby would be enough for her daughter to get her shit together. Sadly, it wasn't. With finality, and a handful of earth, she said her goodbye. Then put one foot in front of the other and carried on. Like she always did.

Akin to the cycle of life and death, time moved in a cyclical nature with the seasons. Granny had always lived off the bounty of the land as much as possible, which in itself was a rotation of never-ending chores. Most of the chores revolved around food. Planting and picking and preparation. After preparation there was planning what's next. That to-do list was made easier with a second set of hands. They were little hands, but hands just the same.

There were some tasks Chicory minded, like picking greens when the stalk's barbs would prick her hands. But boy, they were good for eating. Gran said, 'Poke, collards and even dandelion, but you got to gather it before all that sweetness goes into those perdy yellow blooms.' They'd bubble in a pot on the wood stove all day with a piece of meat Gran had scrounged up. Chic didn't mind the picking too much, because dipping bread in the deep green likker was her favorite meal.

As the days got warmer and longer, the pot on the stove was still bubbling, but now it was a bath for canning jars. "Today's pick will be tomorrow's vittles," Gran said. "We will stock the pantry full up for winter with the garden's vegetables until the tips of our fingers are sore." For all the moaning and groaning Chicory did while canning, Gran would just laugh and say, "Chicory, you just keep up. There'll come a dark day in January when you'll be thankful for a taste of summer."

Those days on the homestead were Chicory's earliest memories. She hung on to Granny's lessons as tight as her apron strings. These teachings the child's mind absorbed in that way growing minds do.

Chicory loved caring for the hens. Gathering eggs in misty mornings, listening to the noises they made, clucking their laying songs.

Granny had taught her work songs to sing, so every task seemed like play to the little girl.

Food to forage in the woods of Appalachia was plentiful. Gran would stuff their pockets with dried rosemary and mint to run off chiggers and ticks when they took to the paths on their land. Berries were the reward for braving the thickets, their juice dark as the blood left on the brambles when they met with skin.

It wasn't just food they gathered. Granny knew her way around a yarb and collected ingredients for the tonics and tinctures to cure the ailments the cold mountain air was sure to bring in. "But just take care, and listen what I tell you. These woods, they are a tricky sort, and for all their bounty, there is just as much around here can make you sick. So, you learn what not to take and what not to eat as well."

Gran's husband had passed ages ago when the black lung consumed him like most men around these parts his age. She'd told him that going into the Earth and taking wasn't right. They had to give something back. That was the natural order of things. You had to make your offerings. He didn't listen and the Earth took its due anyways by taking the lives of the men who went into her mines. Most cases Gran enjoyed being right, but not this time. No, not this time.

They were as self-sufficient as an old woman and child could be. While they could do many things, there were some tasks they couldn't do well. Tasks like chopping enough logs to feed their fire all season long or shoveling snow. Thankfully that's what neighbors were for.

CHAPTER 2

HOME IS WHERE THE HOLLER IS

Up in Chicory and Gran's neck of the woods the roads were often treacherous and steep. There were watch for "fallen rock" signs and "deer crossing" signs. The odds were good someone would hit some wildlife one day, but it never stayed on the side of the road for long—fresh meat attracted too many hungry mouths.

Folks lived in homes of all shapes and sizes, not just run down places with trash filled front porches or automotive lawn ornaments. There were some like that but the people in these hills worked hard for what they had, big or small, whatever it was, it got taken care of. If someone couldn't fix it, sure enough there was someone who would help. Neighbors were always there if needed, and it went both ways.

Granny and Chicory resided in a place called Dark Holler. Probably there were dozens of similarly named hollers all through those parts, flat places that sat between the foothills of the mountains, and those mountains going on in every direction one looked, the trees so dense, they grew right up to the road and over it, shadowing it, giving it the name.

Three properties sat along Dark Holler Lane as it snaked between the hills, where a creek ran alongside it. There was a time there were more people, but the state took their land for their park. Those families got resettled closer to town and folks still talked about it.

Gran's cabin was modest, with a porch big enough for sitting, and a sky-blue front door. Wooden shingles covered its sides like scales. Thankfully, it was built late enough in the century to be wired for electricity and indoor plumbing. Inside there was an open area lit up with light from a few windows. A farmhouse table built by Gran's late husband separated the kitchen from the living room. There was space at one end for eating but the rest was covered with plants and bottles for Gran's workings. Multicolored rag rugs lay over the wood floor and drying bouquets hung from the rafters. A big wood stove sat in the far corner. All-in-all, a cheery and welcoming place.

At the end of the lane, in another modest but well-kept home, Winter and his son Hawk lived. Part of the Cherokee, their tribe was native to the land, and Winter had saved his pay for years to buy back what was rightfully his in the first place. He was a spiritual man and continued many of the traditions of his people. Hunting and fishing the land and letting nothing go to waste. He planted the Three Sisters: corn, beans and squash. He went to the annual Powwow where he purchased beaded jewelry to add to what already clinked together on his wrists and neck, and he made fry bread on weekends. Hawk's ma had passed away a few years back with a sickness too big for mountain cures alone, and by the time they made it to the specialist in the big city, sadly it was too late. Winter had a job doing tree work, so Gran kept an eye on Hawk for him and it gave Chicory someone to play with.

Both were quiet children, but there was a comfort to being quiet together. So as time went on, the two became thick as thieves. They roamed the Holler like it was their own personal playground. Just shy of feral with bare feet and untamed hair, what a sight the two made, heads bent together, conspiring, one black as a starless night and the other light and delicate as cornsilk. It would make Gran smile to see the two of them running to splash in the creek, his mahogany fingers entwined with her pale ones.

It was a rare day the kids would be kept inside; the weather would have to be a right fright to do so. If Hawk and Chicory were thirsty, they would drink from the hose, or the spring on up the mountain. If the two got hungry, they would eat their fill of tomatoes or peaches from Gran's garden. That is, until she caught and chased the two from it, yelling she'd beat the daylights out of them. She didn't mean it of course but Hawk and Chic still ran from her holding their bellies to keep their daylights in, whatever those were.

Sometimes Gran wanted to run an errand without two young'uns in tow. Those days Hawk and Chicory would go to the other neighbor, Widow Mary. Why they didn't call it Widow Holler is not known, but one can only reckon it was too sad.

Widow Mary was curling in on herself with age but still had a long thick braid down her back. The braid had just gone snow white. She had lost her husband to the mines too but was able to keep their land with the small pittance she received monthly. Gran and Chicory were always leaving this and that for her. It was the neighborly way after all.

Widow Mary came from the old country. Her house had curly cues in the corners and thistles carved into the shutters. Truth be told it looked like it was one of those gingerbread houses right out of the big book of faerie tales the woman had. Mary would feed the children shortbread cookies with glasses of milk while she read to them. Their small legs would stick to the plastic covers over the old woman's couch while her thick accent made the stories sound real.

Widow Mary always had milk. She put it in her bird bath for the faeries. Chicory and Hawk never saw one of the wee folk, but Mary sure had a lot of cats. The sight of those lanky felines perched on the edge of the cement bowl lapping dairy brought pure delight to children. Widow Mary swore none of the cats were hers, but she let them inside, though only through the front door. She also bestowed them all with the names of the ancient gods of her ancestors. Hawk and Chicory loved going there even if it was just to hear the woman psp-psping for Dagda, Ceridwen and Aeugus.

Even though the children never saw anything out of the ordinary, that didn't mean they didn't believe. Because when you live far enough into the woods, you find yourself believing in a lot of things. A lot of things you hope you don't ever see.

CHAPTER 3
SUPERSTITIONS, HAINTS, AND HEEBIE-JEEBIES

"In Appalachia you can have your come-to-Jesus every Sunday, but there are still a thousand and one ways to ward off evil," said Gran.

And then Chicory asked, "How do you ward off evil, Gran?" She'd been told before, but always liked to hear her Gran tell it.

Gran obliged, "Always keep a broom by your front door to sweep out evil if it gets in, and if the broom falls ... "

Chicory cried out, "Company's coming you don't want!"

Gran nodded big, and continued. "Make sure your screen door is shut in the first place ... " and waited for Chicory's refrain ...

"Because that will keep out the evil."

And Gran continued, "Sky-blue is a good color for your front door to discourage evil from coming to it. Close your blinds at night ... "

"So evil can't see in!" said Chicory.

"Plant juniper bushes in front of your house because you know what it keeps away?"

"Evil!"

"That's right, evil."

Granny even had glass bottles hanging from the branches of nearby trees to catch bad spirits at night. In the morning, the sun would turn whatever was caught in the bottles to mist while a kaleidoscope of colors danced on the ground below.

Gran passed down these and many other rules to Chicory. Rules that had been written when the earliest of folks settled in the Holler. Rules that will keep one alive in the dense, damp woods. Ancient woods. So old, not even the Lord knew what all resided there.

Gran would say, "You see, you can't live here without seeing some things, hearing some things and experiencing some things you can't explain. It could be just a print in the mud, unlike anything you'd seen before. It could be big and furry, and definitely not a bear or not a deer. Just remember, if you see it—*no you didn't*. Once you acknowledge it, you accept it; and acceptance gives it the power to interact with you and no good ever comes from that. Just mind your business and hope that whatever it is you think you saw does the same. And Haints; Haints are everywhere. Haints can be things of terrors past, shadow people, a swirling mist or simply an unnaturally cool breeze where there ain't oughta be one. Just make sure to turn out your pockets so whatever it is don't follow you home."

Everyone around the Holler had their own beliefs. Widow Mary called the evil Strigies. She had iron horseshoes hanging over her front and back doors and mason jars full of nails buried at each corner of her property. She would remind Chic and Hawk to watch for Pukwudgies. "They love to play tricks So always keep something sweet in your pockets," she'd say. "And stay out of the mushroom rings and pine thickets because you never know where you'll end up."

Winter told Chicory and Hawk about Skinwalkers and the Raven Mocker, and the Moon-Eyed People. Tales so terrifying they caused many sleepless nights. Most of those creatures followed the Trail of Tears feeding off the pain and sadness of the People. What had been done to them was so awful, that no matter where one's feet were planted on the ground, that ground had been stolen, and those who came to understand that, felt deeply the pain and sadness.

And if they caught Gran on a good night, she would tell them about the evil things, and the not so evil things. She would rock back in her chair and recite, "Here in the Holler? Up the mountainside there are Owlmen, Mothmen, and Goatmen. We've got Snallygasters and Snarly Yows, Wampus cats and various dog like monsters. Black things and white things and more Squatches than you've got fingers to count. Creatures that walk on two legs or four and things that slither and things that fly. There are even creatures that just hang out down in the towns like Grafton or Flatwoods. But the caves, they run deeper than anyone dares to go, mile after mile underground. What lives down in those caves there would haunt even your worst nightmare."

"Will we ever see any of these?"

"Oh now keep the broom by the door, and be smart out up the mountain, hopefully you'll never run into anything that means you harm, but your odds are better if you stay on the damn trail. People all have their reasons for seeking the solitude of the outdoors. For us it is for gathering sustenance, for others, they are just wanting to be alone without distractions, only the sound of their own footsteps and the rustling of the trees overhead. Even staying on the trails, they could get lost. Just one good storm can change a path people have marked and have taken a thousand times. If you lose your way after the trail forks, and you've gone the wrong way, it is very easy to get disoriented, every tree starts looking the same. The woods like to trick you like that."

"And when it goes quiet ... the birds, the bugs and squirrels and like ... It's because the little creatures don't want to attract the attention of what's come close. Pay attention to your surroundings and if you get that feeling of being followed, you probably are. And don't let night catch you without some kind of walls and a good fire."

"Granny, you know everything," Chicory would say, loving her stories.

"Oh, well I had good teachers and I listened to them. Around the same time I was learning the alphabet, I was also learning one of the most important rules for survival—passed down from Meemaws and Pappaws for generations—and that is, of all things, about whistling.

> One saying was:
> 'Whistling women and a crowing hen,
>> always come to a no good end.'
> There's also:
> 'Sing at the table or whistle in bed,
>> the devil will get you by the hair on your head.'

"Just don't whistle. Especially in the woods and especially at night. Maybe what I've already mentioned will hear it. Maybe you'll call something else when you whistle," Gran said. "Whistling attracts crawlers. Trust me, you don't ever want to run into one of those."

Granny and her neighbors did their best to make sure Chicory and Hawk were prepared for mountain survival. The things that made sense, and even all those things that might not make sense to some. While most teaching does happen at home, there comes a time in every child's life when they need to learn from others, and for that Chicory and Hawk were sent to school.

CHAPTER 4
PRETTY IS AS PRETTY DOES

There was Downtown, the heart of it, with big old houses built by the men who once owned the mines but didn't do the dirty work. The surrounding brick buildings there had been renovated into fancy shops with handmade crafts and farm-to-table restaurants catering to the tourists the nearby park brought in. Folks that lived there just shook their heads at that, "Ain't all food farm-to-table? Isn't everything made by hand?"

From there, it was just Town, box stores and fast-food chains, with newer built houses in neat rows to make neighborhoods. That was where the school was. Further out, there were the farms and trailer parks. Further still, were the dirt lane kids, the holler kids, kids like Hawk and Chicory who had to wake up at the crack of dawn and get down to the main road for their hour long bus ride.

In the beginning school is easy. It's all fun and games. When you're a child you don't let race or gender or whose momma your momma doesn't like spoil a good time. When you're little you just play. A child doesn't notice whose shoe soles are hanging on for dear life by a piece of duct tape. You all sing the same songs. Play the same games. Everyone is your friend.

That sure doesn't last long, does it?

Hawk could sit and listen to a story his dad would tell or the fairie tales of Widow Mary, but when he had to read himself, the words would jumble when they got to his brain, not making any sense. He couldn't sit still as long as the teachers wanted. He didn't like wearing shoes, so he couldn't concentrate because he kept thinking about taking his shoes off. School was loud, so he'd feel hot and cold at the same time. There were so many distractions, he couldn't focus on one thought before another thought pushed the last one aside. School made Hawk feel like he could crawl out of his own skin. So, he'd get frustrated. When he got frustrated, he got angry. That is how Hawk and Chicory found themselves in different classrooms.

Chicory took to school like a fish in water. As soon as she could string the alphabet together all she wanted to do was read. School was just an ends to a means and a way to get more books and Chic was perfectly content to read or draw and not speak to another soul.

Children have no concept of time. Weeks are broken up by weekends. Months are broken up by summertime and not summertime. Children don't see the years fly by or notice their small bodies as they are stretched and pulled into something resembling what they'll look like when they're grown.

No, children don't notice these things, but time passes whether they're paying attention or not.

Around the age where kids started to want to impress each other, Chicory became the class outcast. While the other girls were trying to look older, Chic dressed like a manic toddler. She wore rainbow knitted sweaters over cat leggings and tie died shirts with howling wolves, completely oblivious to her peers taunting. She would find a corner and sit alone eating Granny packed lunches of egg salad sandwiches and pickled beets. She would hide behind the cover of her latest fantasy book or draw in a sketchbook until she was lost in a world where thrown insults couldn't reach. Drawing was another thing Chicory did with ease and filled books with the wonders of the natural world.

This is also around the age where Chicory's freckles stopped going away over the winter. Patterns of dots marked her entire face and every visible swatch of skin. If this didn't cause enough unwanted attention, her bullies noticed something else. That while her eyes were the bright green of a new spring leaf, the right one was also half brown. It didn't matter that they teased her about this though, because it was one of her favorite things about herself.

Loretta was a girl who noticed Chicory. Being a pariah herself, the two would often pair with each other for dreaded group assignments. Loretta was a girl with her own share of bullies. While Chicory stood out like a sore thumb for being eccentric, Etta was cursed with early development. During adolescence, when girls started being mean to each other out of jealousy, nothing caused jealousy more than a pair of breasts. All the boys liked her too much and all the girls not enough.

Loretta was bullied coming and going. She was called a kiss ass for being a teacher favorite because she was smart and polite. She was called ugly and fat because she was the complete opposite, with auburn hair most girls had to get from a box and a complexion unmarked by puberty.

It didn't help that Etta came from piss-poor means in the trailer park. Her momma, bless her heart, was a hopeless romantic. She'd fallen for one too many knights in shining armor who were going to rescue her from poverty. But all her momma got was a broken heart, another baby, and a reputation in their small town.

Etta didn't know her father. She had been born on the wrong side of the blanket. Her momma said he ran off and that was that. Etta watched her momma struggle and didn't care a wit about boys, in fact she didn't trust them as far as she could throw them. Her daydream was living in a house with a foundation and a second floor. A house with stairs is what Etta dreamed of.

Most of Etta's fantasies were inspired by the massive white farmhouse she could see from the back of her family's double wide. The farm property butted right to the trailer park with a barbed wire fence between the two for the grazing cows. The farmhouse had a wraparound porch dotted with wicker rocking chairs. Etta longed for a glimpse inside. That, and a friend.

Etta had been orbiting Chicory for weeks when she finally asked, "Doesn't it bother you? The things they all say?"

Chicory looked up from her sketching at Loretta, completely perplexed, and asked, "Who?"

Laughing nervously Loretta asked, "Can we be friends?"

"I didn't realize we weren't," Chicory answered easily, because it was the God's honest truth.

Etta had a friend.

While the two girls couldn't have been more different, they got along just fine. They complimented each other and were both sharp as tacks. Etta accepted that she got Hawk as a bonus friend because Hawk and Chicory were two peas in a pod. He even let the girls braid his long hair and paint his toenails. Mr. Winter came to help Etta's ma by repairing things that needed fixing around their trailer. He and Granny would always have extra from their gardens to give Etta and her brothers too. And while Hawk would always be Chicory's heart and soul, Chic could admit sometimes a girl just needed another girl to talk to. Chicory couldn't share all her secrets with Hawk, especially since some of her secrets were about him.

CHAPTER 5
BY THE SKIN OF THEIR TEETH

All week it had been raining cats and dogs. Which was why, before the sun started to rise, Hawk was in Chicory's bedroom bright eyed and bushy tailed dressed to hike. He couldn't stand heavy boots but got by just fine in worn sneakers.

Hawk had a knit cap pulled over his head, with two long braids snaking out over each shoulder, as he dragged Chic out of her warm bed. Groaning, she threw on her jeans and a sweater. Getting up this early only meant one thing, they were going to look for morels. Granny was awake, all ready to start the day's tasks, and sent them off with fresh biscuits and a kiss on their cheeks.

Fog thickened the air like a dream. They could barely see the few feet in front of them. Luckily, the nearby trails were as familiar to the two as the backs of their hands.

Chicory should've known Hawk would be right about the day being good for mushroom hunting. Just after entering the shelter of the trees, they were treated to the blue green phosphorescent light of foxfire. Poisonous to eat, but beautiful to look at and not often seen. Rare as the sight was, that wasn't what they were after, and it did little to improve Chicory's mood.

Hawk and Chicory trekked all the way to the river. It was a mile past their families' property lines into what was protected park land. They had passed the sign posted about half an hour before. It was by the river the two found a felled oak bursting with their quarry. Covered by a tea towel, their baskets were practically full of the mushroom's honeycomb like heads.

"Don't forget to leave the roots," Hawk reminded Chic.

"I know, I know," Chic yawned. It was too early for this; the trees grew so close together in this part, it was still dark, like the sun hadn't even risen yet. Not to mention, it was colder than a witch's tit and Chicory was tired of being chilly and damp. It was making her even more irritable.

Chicory was just about to complain when she noticed Hawk had gone still. His shoulders, which had widened out this last year, were tense. Matter of fact everything had gone still. The woods were silent. But there, creeping into Chicory's bones, was the sneaking suspicion they were not alone. There were pressure points on her skin where eyes touched it. It was not uncommon to sense this and never see what was watching her, though the feeling still gave her goose bumps.

They both held their breath and subtly scanned their surroundings. Neither wanted to acknowledge whatever was out here with them and both hoped whatever it was would just move on. Hawk's eyes met Chicory's and he nodded. As silently as possible they both took out their pocket knives. No one went out there without a knife. Just in case.

The slushing sound of wet leaves drew their attention. Chicory gasped the moment she saw it. She couldn't help herself. Because there, on the other side of the river, stood a pale, white creature. No, not a creature. A girl, naked as the day she was born. A dirty girl, thin as a rail. Her long, stringy hair was full of leaves and brambles. Her bare breasts peeking through the tangled mess.

"Are you lost?" Chicory asked softly. "What's your name?"

The girl tilted her head to the side like she was trying to get a better listen. That movement seemed ... off. But not as off-putting as her eyes. Her eyes were completely solid black—no white or colored irises—just two dark yawning pits. Ice cold terror replaced the blood in Chic's veins.

"Chic, we need to get out of here, now!" Hawk whispered and grabbed Chicory's arm. The girl creature made a sound in her throat. It grated, like two rocks rubbing together.

"Hawk, what is she? A Stigie?" The creature's skin was so pale it was almost translucent, Chic could see the tendrils of blue veins underneath.

"It's one of the Moon-Eyed People. They usually don't stray this far from the caves. This one is young, maybe it's lost," Hawk answered. It was his ancestors that had pushed them into those caves hundreds of years ago.

"Should we help her?" Chicory started to ask but Hawk cut her off.

"Stay away from it," Hawk warned and pulled Chic closer, his fingers digging into the flesh of her arm. "Don't go anywhere near that thing."

The creature's throat-grinding got louder until it was [sounded] like a growl. It inhaled deeply to taste them on the air. It was getting agitated, not being able to cross the running water to get at them.

Hawk and Chicory moved slowly away, never putting their backs to the creature.

Once out of its sight, they took off running and didn't stop until they broke through the tree line. Bent over, hands on their knees, they tried to catch their breath. That had been a close one.

The creature watched its prey scurry away. Usually, it could lure the males too busy looking at its naked form to notice teeth until it was too late. The colony never came this far. They had their own rules, but the creature had grown bored and often wandered. Its wandering had on many occasions been fruitful. It had tasted flesh and fear, and it was always hungry. At home the young ones were only given scraps. Away from the others the creature could feast. Alone it could gorge itself on the hot steaming things inside a living body. It could be the one to hunt. To kill. To bloodlust.

The sun was getting higher, the creature would be blind soon. It had to get back to the caves. Luckily on the way it spied a flash of bright color. An early morning hiker making their way down a trail, completely unaware. The muscles in the creature's face moved to what would be a smile on a human, but on its face, it was a thing of cruelty.

The hiker screamed.

CHAPTER 6
FIT TO BE TIED

Emory Green swung his long legs as they dangled from where he sat on the rocky overlook. He had strayed from the other Scouts, claiming he had to piss like a racehorse, but in truth he wanted some peace. Just shy a few patches from Eagle Scout, he was one of three leaders supervising an overnight primitive camp out. He had camped in this particular spot dozens of times and was familiar with the surrounding foot trails. And this was how Emory found himself watching the sun streak pink and orange through the sky, while it made its way behind the mountain range. He knew he had to get back before dark, but he also needed a little more time with this view.

Emory had a lot on his mind for a boy about to start his first year of high school. There was this thing only Emory knew about himself, and everyone around him was totally fooled by it. That thing was this: Emory was a liar. It hadn't started that way, when he was a young boy, he went along with whatever his family wanted, because that's what good boys do. And Emory was a good boy. He had always been big boned and now his already man-sized body made him indispensable on the football field. He had spent years of Friday nights under the field lights with his best friend and the team's quarterback Tommy. But as the summer's end was imminent and practice was to start next week, the only thing Emory could think about was how much he hated football.

Emory also lied to his parents when he pretended to want to take over the cattle farm like the last three generations of Emory's before him. He lied to God every Sunday when he pretended to pray, but was counting down the minutes until he could go home to his bedroom. He lied to the whole damn town when they talked about the upcoming football season. He lied to Tommy about how excited he was to start at the high school because he actually didn't even like Tommy (or any of the other guys he had grown up with anymore). His group of friends cared more about popularity than anything and sacrificed too many feelings to climb the social ladder. Worst of all, Emory lied to himself when he let these friends tease and bully others while he stood by and watched. He had let the lying go on so long he didn't even know who the real Emory was.

"Where to even begin?" he wondered as the dark started to get a little darker and he knew even he wouldn't be able to find his way back without a light. As he left the overlook to make his way back to the campsite, he heard a whistle coming from the trees to his side. It didn't sound like it was from the direction of the other Scouts, and his Poppop told him long ago, never whistle while in the woods. Emory ignored it and hiked back a little faster, deciding right then tonight's fireside tale would have something to do about whistling. Tonight, he had a dozen boys to scare. Tomorrow he would do something even scarier, he'd start telling the truth.

Downtown on Main Street sat a variety store of sorts. The store was full of trinkets and odds and ends, it was a favorite among tourists. Chicory was in this particular place when she noticed a boy from her class. She recognized him instantly as the boy next door (next door to Etta to be exact). She watched as he stared at a Sasquatch shirt like it held the secrets of the Universe. She was planning to walk by unannounced but something about his agonized look made her stop and speak. "That's a great tshirt."

Emory jumped at the sound of her voice, as distinguishable as her freckled skin. Deep and raspy as it was, it belonged to Chicory, who he knew from school.

"I'm deciding if it's what I'll spend my birthday money on," he explained, though it went much deeper than that. How could he explain that wearing this shirt would be the first time he ever truly expressed himself. He loved the artwork but also, he saw himself in the Sasquatch. Like him, the creature was big and shy and loved the forest.

"If you like Squatches there are some fun books at the bookstore next door. That's where I usually spend my birthday money," Chicory suggested.

"What are you doing here anyways?" Emory asked, but chided himself for sounding rude. "Sorry, that came out wrong."

"It's okay," Chicory laughed it off. "My Granny makes the candles and soaps they sell here. We're just dropping off new stock."

Emory wondered then how much you just don't know about a person.

Chicory smiled, "Okay then, have fun. You should get that," she said, touching the shirt, lightly, "the green leaves will match your eyes." She threw the words over her shoulder as she glided away, her pale hair floating behind her. Emory's ears turned red with the compliment, and he hoped no one noticed. In the end he got the shirt.

He wore his new garment like a shield as he peddled his bike the few miles to his Coach's house. Standing on the front porch, Coach hung his head as Emory explained why he was quitting the team. Blah blah schoolwork, blah blah something else, all the Coach heard was goodbye undefeated Championship.

It was as if a weight had lifted off his chest. Emory smiled wide as he bicycled his way back home. Unfortunately, the phone had already been ringing off the hook. Coach had called his parents and then called all the other parents of his teammates.

"You didn't ask me if you could quit," Emory's mother shouted. He had barely stepped inside the house before she descended on him, hands on her wide hips.

"I didn't realize you were the one playing," Emory fired back. Good mood now long gone, he earned a gasp from his mother.

"Emory Green!" she screamed like a banshee. "You sassing me? You're fit to be tied, boy. What has gotten into you?"

Emory Sr. had heard his wife's screeching from the back cow field. Whatever in tarnation was going on, it wasn't good. The screen door banged when he entered, drawing her attention away from their child. She exclaimed, "Your son quit the football team!"

"Dad, I just don't want to play anymore. I hate it," Emory pleaded with his father, who could admit his son had looked a little forlorn lately. He had chalked it up to hormones.

"Okay," Emory Sr. shrugs. He's always been a man of few words, preferring to cut to the chase. He then moved into the kitchen for a glass of sweet tea.

The missus followed him, still whooping and hollering.

"So what?" he replied, calmly. "He doesn't want to play football. Let it go. At this point you're just beating a dead horse."

His wife stared at him, her mouth wide open and gaping like a caught fish. Her husband had always just agreed with her. Had every man in her life lost their damn minds?

Sighing, Emory Sr. pulled his wife into arms thick with muscles from a lifetime of farming. The sweet scent of hay on his skin as she breathed him in calmed her.

"Em's a good boy. He'll be just fine. Besides, now we got our Friday nights free," he joked as he nuzzled her neck. She smacked him away, laughing. She let out a sigh that was long and suffering, but she conceded.

Rubbing his hands together and satisfied this ordeal was behind them, he asked, "Now, what's for dinner?"

CHAPTER 7
THAT DOG WON'T HUNT

By the time the first day of high school came around, it was evident by the cold shoulders that Emory was useless to his so-called friends if he wasn't playing on the team. It was alright though. Emory felt happier than ever. No friends were better than those guys, and it was fine and dandy, until he found himself standing in the lunchroom. All eyes had turned to him to see where he would sit.

His ears were turning red with embarrassment. Just as he was about to bolt and eat his lunch in the library, he heard the voice of an angel.

"You can sit with us, Em," Loretta called.

Em. Only his parents had ever called him that. It sounded so intimate coming from this girl he barely knew but had lived next door to his whole life. Her auburn hair shone copper under the harsh fluorescent lights of the cafeteria. Loretta waved him over while Hawk and Chicory looked on.

He was tense at first. Emory didn't have much experience with girls. He marveled at how at ease Hawk was around them. Luckily the girls did most of the talking. As luck would also have it, both girls were in his classes the rest of the day.

"Guess you're one of the freaks now?" Tommy said in the hall as he bumped past Emory aggressively. It didn't bother him as much as he thought it would.

"Yeah, guess I am," Emory chuckled.

Over the coming weeks Emory realized the girls were smart. Really smart. With Hawk, Em could talk about the outdoors and trails he was familiar with. Hawk didn't know his way around the classroom well, but his knowledge of the outside world was incredible. The two boys found their common ground there and went hiking and fishing together. Emory was discovering there were different kinds of smart. He wasn't exactly sure how he fit, but fit he did, and that's how Emory found his truth.

With the crisp fall weather came deer season. It was chilly the morning Emory and his father took to their property to hunt. Emory carried the rifle he'd gotten a few Christmases past though he'd never killed a thing with it. The rifle hadn't been fired since that first Christmas morning. Father and son walked companionably through the trees. The leaves had turned red, orange and brown and fell around them like rain.

It wasn't long until the two heard a rustle, not loud enough to be a deer, most likely a squirrel. Out from the brush a little beagle crawled looking like eight miles of bad road. Emory crouched down to seem more approachable, and approach the little dog did. It was shivering, whining and covered in scratches and engorged ticks. Emory poured some of his water for the dog, who lapped it up thirstily. Despite the dog's disheveled state, which upon further inspection was a girl, Em tucked her inside his coat. She stunk to high heaven, but the comfort and warmth of his body calmed her down instantly.

"Where do you think she came from?" Emory asked his dad.

Emory Sr. shook his head. "Probably got left, nothing worse than a dog that won't hunt," he replied in his low timbre. "Most likely, too friendly, so she wasn't any use."

Sadly, Emory stroked her small head. Even dirty her ears were velvety soft. The little dog stared up at him with all the trust in the world. She was falling in love already. So was he.

"Being nice is not useless," Emory whispered. Just because your heart was meant for something other than what someone else planned for you, did not make you useless. "Please let me keep her," he pleaded.

Emory Sr. looked at his son. His son, who never asked for much, but was looking at him with the same eyes as that lost puppy. "Fine. But you gotta deal with your mother."

With the little dog now in tow, both father and son decided to just call it a day and head back home. They had barely begun to trek back when they spotted a deer just a few yards in front of them, which was weird, because they hadn't heard it crunching through the leaves.

"Em." His father's voice was stern, and he had put his arm out to stop Emory from walking any further. The little dog started to whine just as the deer lifted its head to look at them. It was like something else was pretending to be a deer, but just not getting it right. The almost deer looked at them from eyes that were too forward facing, on a head that was too round. The jaw on this thing was square and saliva poured from its misshapen mouth like a spigot. The body seemed normal until you got to the legs. Its hind legs were backwards and the deer like creature had joints that were way too big for it. As if the thing wasn't terrifying enough, it stood up on its backwards hind legs and shuffled towards them.

"What the hell is that?" Emory asked breathlessly.

His Dad aimed his shotgun at the thing and cocked it. "Alright we don't want any trouble. So go on back to wherever you came from," he yelled, never taking his gun off the creature, while saying to Emory, "It's a Not Deer. Seen one other with your Granddaddy many moons ago."

"But what is it?" Emory asked, confused.

"All I know, Son, is that it's like a deer but it's not." All that explanation did was leave Emory with more questions.

It felt like longer, but the Not Deer left them alone and walked like a human back into the trees, it's forelegs dangling uselessly as it shuffled. When all trace of it was gone, they high tailed it home, hearts racing the whole time.

Em named the little dog Fern after the plants that grow wild on the trail she was found on. After a bath, even his mother agreed Fern cleaned up rather nice.

His father didn't bring up their experience, but curious minds knew where to find answers—the library.

CHAPTER 8
BE CAREFUL WHAT YOU WISH FOR

Emory had always been a curious boy, too curious for his own good, if you asked his mother. Curiosity may have killed the cat, but without it how would we ever learn? And learning was Emory's favorite.

After his encounter with the Not Deer, Em searched for answers in the school library. He didn't find much there but he was introduced to the "par-a-normal" and the "supernatural." The literature he found set into motion a fervor that he would have for the rest of his life.

On Wednesdays, Grandma Faye, who was Grandmother to Etta's youngest two brothers, would pick up all of the boys and take them to Mickey D's. That woman smoked like a chimney but was worth her weight in gold for all the help she gave. So, Wednesdays became library day. Etta, Emory, Chicory and Hawk would walk the few blocks from the school and Chic's Granny would pick them up in her decrepit pick up a few hours later. The boys would hop in the truck's bed for the ride.

Hawk tagged along, not interested in anything there but Chicory, who would spend the entire time in the fantasy shelves.

Etta, who had vowed not to date until after high school and swore she didn't believe in love anyway, picked novels whose covers were adorned with half naked men.

"Deflowered by the Duke?" The librarian held up a title that promised to be a bodice ripper, "Aren't you a little young for

this?" she asked, while glaring down at Etta from behind the counter. She moved to scan another title, "*Married to the Mafia King*? Really Etta?"

Two spots of pink colored Etta's cheeks. She was a terrible liar. "They're for my Momma. She's sick, you know?" They were for her Momma, she was just going to read them as well, so she wasn't technically lying.

The librarian visibly softened. Being as small of a town as this town was, everyone knew about Etta's mother. That woman hadn't left their double-wide in years and all the gossip known came from the local in-home nurse who cared for her. "Well in that case ... " the librarian said, before handing over the goods.

Thanks to the local folklore section in the county library, Emory found his answers and then some. So many unexplained creatures and happenings and disappearances were right here in the very mountains he loved. Could there really be monsters out there? Well, he'd seen one with his very own eyes, hadn't he?

Emory read every close encounter, every recorded sighting, and every tale of disappearance he could find. Normally he kept his passion to himself, but he had just gotten an illustrated book of Cryptids and couldn't think of anything else.

On this particular day it was just him and Chicory at the lunch table. Etta was retaking a quiz and Hawk was in detention. Chic had her face buried in her own book, so he didn't feel rude reading his.

However, the beautiful art on the pages caught Chic's eye and she found herself reading the book upside down.

"My neighbor calls them Owlmen," she said around bites of her sandwich.

"That's the Mothman," Emory perked up, hopeful he could talk about Cryptids with someone else.

"Look the same to me," she shrugged. "They're usually out on the ridge just past the Knob, especially in the summer—they love blackberries," Chicory explained, like seeing a giant shaggy monster with wings was completely natural.

"Wait. You've seen him?" Emory asked incredulously, his heart beating faster. Seeing another creature would be a wish come true.

"Yeah, like I said, we've always called them Owl Folk. If you don't mind them, they won't mind you," Chicory explained. It came to Emory's attention that she was eating what appeared to be a green bean sandwich. He raised a brow, so she ripped him a corner off. "Dilly beans," she shrugged.

"Have you seen anything else in the book," he asked, hopeful, as she fingered through the pages. He tasted the morsel she had given him, and the sour tang surprised him, though not in a bad way.

"No, nothing else."

He tried to hide his disappointment.

"Maybe this ... one." She tapped her finger on the snarling face of the Sheepsquatch. "Looks a lot like a White Thang but you'd have to ask Hawk. They stay in high elevations, so I've only caught a glimpse from far away. Your book doesn't have any Moon-Eyed People in it."

Holding his breath, he thought back on his research. No, he'd never heard of those before. "What are they?" he asked.

"They're all in the caves around here. One followed me and Hawk just a ways back. Scared the bejesus out of us. I thought it was someone lost til I got a good look at its eyes," she explained.

"Can you take me there?" Excitement coursed through him.

"I don't think that's a good idea. Folks go missing out there way too often for my liking. The park blames the terrain but ... " she trailed off.

"I'm going, with or without you." Mind made up, Emory was going monster hunting.

"Going where?" Etta asked, as she joined the table.

"He's going to get himself killed," Chicory answered.

"It's just a little adventure, that's all," he said excitedly, but the girls were not so sure.

Hawk was wrangled into the adventure because there was no way in hell Chicory was going without him. His condition was: the trips had to be during the brightest parts of the day. (Like that meant anything in the deepest parts of the woods.) Etta was going too, for fear of missing out, and planned days the boys would stay with Grandma Faye. Fern tagged along because she followed Emory around everywhere he went.

Emory used his Scout teachings and orchestrated their hikes on a map. He narrowed down a handful of possibilities. The opening they were looking for would have to be on the opposite side of the entrance used for tourists. The Moon-Eyed People couldn't be more than a few miles from Dark Holler. The group decided to cross the river where Hawk and Chicory had seen one.

The first cave was the closest to the main trails. It looked to be mostly used for partying since the cave was full of discarded beer bottles and graffiti. The second cave was a little farther out. The ammonia smell hit them before they even entered. This cave was full of bats.

Three is a magic number, mystical and powerful, so it shouldn't have come as a surprise they would find what they were looking for in the third cave. This hike had been the most strenuous of the three. The trail went up and up by switchbacks and was so narrow in some sections they had to walk single file. Emory wore Fern over his shoulders like a shawl, afraid his dog would fall over the steep side. Once they reached the top, the path flattened out before descending down the other side, where the trail forked. According to Emory's map the trail boasted an overlook to the valley below if they went right. While to the left they'd eventually come to a waterfall and ultimately the next possible cave location.

Water trickled from the wall of rock that rose around them and trees jutted out sporadically. They heard the sound of insects as they rounded a bend and came upon a crevice.

Though the droning of wings grew deafening, they didn't see any bugs. "Where is that noise coming from?" Etta asked over the cacophony.

"Over here," Chicory called from their right. "It's a sink hole." The stench of rot and offal was so strong it made their eyes water. Bile rose in their throats. Back on her four paws, Fern whined and hunched low to the ground with her tail between her legs.

"I can't go any further. I'm going to be sick." Etta bent at the waist, retching. A reflection of light caught her eye as she hurled up the contents of her stomach. On the ground was a piece of jewelry, matted hair crusted with dried blood stuck to it. "We need to get out of here now," she blurted.

But Emory, foolish Emory, made his way to the crevice in the rock. "I'll be quick." And he stepped through.

Hawk sighed and followed.

Choosing to follow their instincts instead of the boys, Chicory stood close to Etta who now held the frightened puppy in her arms. They waited just a few feet away from the entrance.

The opening was just wide enough for Hawk and Emory and their backpacks. They made their way from the hall-like walk-through to a small cavern. Dripping water echoed alongside the scuffing of their shoes. The darkness so opaque, the beams of their flashlights barely penetrated the black. Small rock formations shot up from the damp floor, giving the impression the two were in a gaping mouth.

"Alright, you saw it. Let's go. We shouldn't be here," Hawk said, his sixth sense trying to get his common sense in the same boat. Just as Hawk pulled Emory back the way they had come, he heard it, low and menacing—an unmistakable growl.

A flash of white in their peripheral vision was there and gone too fast for a good look. Rushing towards the exit, they were almost to the walk-through when a hand reached out and yanked Emory's pack. Fear like he'd never known sliced through him, he released the bag from his back and continued racing to get out. Whatever was following them screeched when they flew out of the opening, practically running straight into Etta and Chic. Without a word they pulled the girls into a run as well, not stopping until they crested the mountain into sunlight.

"Did it follow us?" Emory gasped; he could not catch his breath. Black spots floated in his vision. He imagined if he passed out now, he'd surely be caught.

"Can we please go on?" Etta begged, her teeth chattering she was so scared. She was facing away from where they'd run, but

Chicory was not, and swore she saw a familiar pale figure in the shadows between the trees.

The walk home was quiet except for their heavy footfalls. They didn't stop to rest. Emory cradled his dog so she wouldn't slow them down with her exploration. Getting home before dark was their only priority at the moment.

Tears ran down Etta's face. She didn't think she would ever be able to go into the woods again, let alone sleep.

Hawk just kept berating himself the whole way home. He knew better. They could have been killed.

Chicory wondered if the creature was like them and felt love. Did it have friends or a family? Were we just food to them like a deer was to us?

Adrenaline pulsed through Emory's veins. He should have been more scared, but now that they were safe he was exhilarated. Nothing would ever drag him away from these woods, this land and her mysteries. He vowed to the very forest to protect her and her creatures. He also vowed to protect unsuspecting victims from these creatures as well ... for the rest of his life.

CHAPTER 9
HOTTER THAN A SINNER IN CHURCH

It was a summer for the record books. Hotter than blue blazes, even the storms that raged nightly couldn't cool the air down. Raindrops hit the earth and sizzled to steam. The air was so thick you could cut it with a knife. Even the bugs weren't biting.

Most of the workforce had collars of blue and those poor souls working outside came home rode hard and put away wet. It was miserable.

Despite the temperature, Summer can be miserable for a child who sees school as a sanctuary. Maybe their pantry is not stocked at home and their bellies growl all season. Maybe their kin's always yelling and fighting and taking a switch to them.

Or maybe, like Etta, summers were hard because at home there was just so much work.

Etta's momma Jolene had always wondered why she was so easily thrown aside like garbage. All she wanted was to be a keeper to someone. To experience that great love. She'd find love and it was slow dancing in the kitchen to country music. Love was a bubbling crock pot and apple pie in the oven. Love was giggles heard behind her closed bedroom door. But when love was lost, Momma Jo would lay in her bed all day crying over pint after pint of ice cream, and heartsick from being unwanted yet again.

Early puberty had put her in a full-figured body before she had reached double digits. She had been belittled by her folks for being a big girl and had not been allowed dessert after supper. The body shaming didn't stop her from eating. Matter of fact, it had the opposite effect, it made her sad and when she was sad, she looked to food for comfort. By her teenage years Jo had no self-esteem at all, until a man old enough to be her daddy made her feel beautiful by whispering sweet nothings in her ear. His words coaxed her into his arms and then ultimately his bed. He got what he wanted, but the baby they made he did not want.

Each baby Jo birthed left her with a few more pounds than the last, until she was too embarrassed to even leave the house. Most days she stayed in her room and the bathroom attached to it, often sleeping the day away entirely. On good days though, she would have enough clarity to remember that there were five little hearts that beat with love for her and on those good days it was enough.

Now being limited to what she could do because of her size, if Jo couldn't do a task from her bed, she would rely on Etta to do it for her. Cooking, cleaning and shopping fell on the shoulders of the young girl. Etta also made sure her brothers were clean and did their homework. At a time when other teenagers were just starting to think about their futures, Etta had the responsibility of a grown woman. Some days the weight of it threatened to crush her; but in the end it made her very, very strong.

The creek that followed Dark Holler Lane fed into a river, blessedly far enough from the homes that the structures were spared from flooding. The trail Hawk and Chicory most often took into the woods wound alongside that river. Far enough away to feel like another world, but close enough to still hear when suppers called, sat a swimming hole. Winter had been taking those two since they were knee high to a grasshopper, but now that they were older they would venture there alone.

In addition to being the hottest summer on record, Hawk's blood boiled for another reason. Hawk had always considered himself a simple guy. He had no dreams of making his mark on the world. Hawk just wanted to exist in a place that was as uncomplicated as himself. When teachers asked him what he wanted to be when he grew up, he'd simply reply, "Outside." He didn't care how he made his means as long as it was enough to keep a roof over his head when he needed one.

Hawks' future always had Chicory in it. He could remember the very first day they'd met. Her two-toned eyes were rimmed with heavy lashes the same color of her hair. Her eyelashes reminded him of spiderwebs in the light. Hawk had never met anyone as interesting to look at than Chicory. As she acquired more and more freckles, it wasn't until he became a teenage boy that he began to fantasize about the freckles in places that teenage boys fantasize about. He had begun to realize he didn't think she was just interesting to look at, she was the most beautiful thing he had ever seen. This summer Hawk lay in bed awake almost every night heated to his core.

Chicory sprawled over a large boulder, half submerged in the cool water, and tried to ignore Hawk watching her every move. She also tried, but failed, to ignore the fact that he didn't have a shirt on.

His skin color deepened with sun and as he floated in the water next to her, Hawk was thinking about how her skin looked against his. His thoughts surprised him even more when he began to wonder how many different ways they'd mix in children. He could see it perfectly. They would just stay together forever. He had always loved Chic, and he always would.

Hawk interrupted the quiet by voicing his thoughts. "You think it will always be like this?" he asked.

Chicory laughed, "I don't think your future wife would like that very much." Her arm laid over her eyes as she continued to lounge.

Hawk couldn't help himself as he said, "Well I reckon we'll have to get hitched ourselves then." His heart laid bare, and beating so loud, he figured the whole damn woods could hear it like a war drum.

Chicory moved her arm so she could look at him. She had braided his hair in two long braids, his hair black and shiny more like a crow's wing than his namesake. His tawny eyes were her favorite color. Hawk had never lied to her, and she was sure he wasn't going to start now. "Yeah, I reckon we will," She answered softly, and that was that.

Hawk approached her slowly, he didn't want to frighten her away, and sealed the deal with a chaste kiss on the lips.

They held hands walking back home to answer the dinner bell. They hadn't done that since they were little. This time the air charged with a new buzzing energy between them. The rest of the summer they practiced kissing often, but that was it, there wasn't a rush. They had forever, after all.

CHAPTER 10
THERE'S A FOX IN THE HENHOUSE

You can't spend every day with a girl and not learn there are a few of those days each month you leave them the hell alone. So, when Hawk spied Chicory stomping furiously towards the woods with a book in one hand and an entire six pack of chocolate Snack Paks in the other, he decided to leave her to it. She was obviously headed to their spot and didn't want company.

Chicory, being a teenage girl, paid no mind to the chatter of old folks. If she did, she would have known how many days they'd been without rain. So many, the river had dwindled down to a trickle, the riverbed was even starting to grow grass, the water had gotten so low.

But she was lost in her own world, completely unaware of what was going on around her. Oblivious or unworried that the swimming hole was just a puddle of mud, she sat on her favorite rock reading her book and eating pudding.

Just as she was about to find out what it meant to be "ravished by a pirate" (thanking Etta for letting her borrow this particular title), she realized she was squinting to see the words. The woods had gotten dark. Hours had flown by, and it was much later than she normally stayed out, so she hurriedly gathered her things.

At the snap of a twig, Chicory's head swiveled further into the trees. The snap echoed louder than it should have. With a stomach-sinking realization there wasn't any other noise, Chicory's searching eyes found the Moon Girl standing a few feet away.

Chicory had been lulled into security by watery sounds of the running river. The river was the only reason she felt safe coming back into the woods after their previous adventures. One glance at the creature's feet covered in mud was all it took for Chicory to understand how wrong she had been. In her teenage ignorance she'd gotten too comfortable and now she'd pay the ultimate price.

The creature's mottled skin at dusk was gray, like some kind of insect larvae. Her hair was longer and dirtier than Chic remembered. The long white filthy tendrils were packed with forest detritus. She was close enough that Chicory could smell the putrid stink of spoiled milk wafting off the monstrous girl.

Chicory would never make it if she ran.

Not taking her eyes off the predator, Chicory felt around for a rock big enough to use as a weapon. Just as her fingers closed around one not as smooth as the others, the Moon Girl jerked forward faster than humanly possible. Chicory belted out a blood curdling scream as she was grabbed, and razor-sharp nails buried into the soft flesh of her upper arms. The creature opened its mouth to rip out Chicory's throat, hot decaying breath and spittle rushes out from behind sharp teeth. Without hesitation Chicory smashed the rock as hard as she could into the side of the creature's face with a sickening thud.

The Moon Girl loosened its grip just long enough for Chicory to scramble to her feet and run. She sprinted as fast as she could, avoiding any tree roots growing onto the trail. Legs and heart pounding, she was forced into a jerking stop by her long hair, which was wrapped around the fist of the walking nightmare. Chicory was thrown to the forest floor, the green briars and underbrush snagged at her clothes and pierced her exposed skin, further inhibiting any escape.

As if it could not get more horrifying, half of the monster's face was now mauled around the eye where Chicory hit. Stony growls emanated from the creature's throat as it crawled up Chicory's body and straddled its reeking naked figure over Chic.

The creature would gut her in a minute, it enjoyed playing with its food. The captive convulsed with fear as the creature dripped saliva on her face.

Hawk thought he was too late as he barreled full speed into the Moon Girl, knocking it off of Chicory's body and into the surrounding thorny brush. *Please be alive.* His only coherent thought as he scooped Chicory into his arms and ran.

Burying her face into Hawk's neck, Chicory breathed him in. Knowing she was safe, her body gave in, and Chicory welcomed the black that washed over her as she passed out.

The creature didn't follow, it was too hurt to fight the strong one. Chicory would have five (ironically crescent shaped) scars on each upper arm to remind her what happened when you got too comfortable in the woods and let your guard down. And the Moon Girl would always carry the mark on her face where Chicory fought back, but worse, the creature would carry a grudge—and the hope—that one day it'd come across the girl that got away, and get her back.

Granny had come out the back door just in time to see Hawk shooting fast as lightning towards Chicory's scream. She waited the hour-long minutes until Hawk broke through the tree line carrying Chicory's unconscious form. She covered her mouth as she sobbed.

Hawk answered her unspoken question. "She's just passed out."

Granny held the screen door open and ushered him inside. "Put her on the couch." She started boiling water, then collected yarbs for a tea for Chicory's nerves and a healing salve for her wounds.

"I can't ... " he replied and sat down, still cradling Chicory's body, his grip tight. Blood trickled down the cuts on her arms onto his own. He didn't notice.

Granny nodded in understanding. She worked slowly but efficiently with the plants she'd gathered. God, she was tired. Lately, it seemed she was the kind of tired that could only be cured by sleeping forever. But she'd been holding on. Holding on for Chicory. But as she watched Hawk tremble as he stroked her granddaughter's hair, it was evident that Chicory would be taken care of.

She took a deep breath. Maybe she could let go.

CHAPTER 11
THE KNOCKING

When Death comes knocking at your door,
don't fret too much my dear.

Just go on and invite him in - he's practically kin,
and nothing you should fear.

Put on the kettle and make some tea.
Is he here for you?
Is he here for me?
Don't really matter much, you see.

Be hospitable, cause just like an old friend,
Death's sure to come calling
again and again.

Chicory had been giving the woods wide berth since her last
encounter. Besides, Granny had been sleeping in later than
usual, so Chic took up more of the household chores. Granny
had always looked old; it was a different matter to see her frail.
All of her joints had started to protrude more prominently
under her paper-thin skin.

The day the unwanted visitor came, Granny proclaimed
she was under the weather and went to have a lay-in. The
feeling that something wasn't right began to creep up on
Chicory and she found herself repeatedly checking on
Granny's sleeping form. She'd release the breath she didn't

realize she was holding every time she went in the bedroom and heard Granny's soft snores.

That "something ain't right" feeling perched on Chic's shoulders like a little bird watching her anxiously work. Chicory checked on the garden. She swept the floor and put the broom back by the front door when she was done. She put a kettle on for tea. The cup of lavender and chamomile blend she steeped to calm her nerves was poised at her lips when the broom fell. The chair scraped loudly across the floor as she pushed it back to stand.

Knock. Knock.

Hawk never knocked, Chicory thought as she opened the door to answer. At the sight of the empty front porch, all the blood drained from Chicory's body. In that instant she knew who was calling.

Death.

All the signs had been there to warn Chicory of what was coming. She saw them and she had been taught what they meant, but deep in her heart she didn't want to admit it to herself.

First it was the owl. For the past three nights the bird hoo-hooed it's lament directly outside of her window. The harbinger of bad news, the owl had come to tell her, "Be ready, he's coming."

Then it was the picture frame. Chicory was dusting when she found Granny and Pap's wedding photo lying face down on the mantle. No open window draft, no mouse passing through, and no particular reason for the sepia tinted photo of a woman and man on their wedding day to fall over.

Chicory tiptoed to the back bedroom. The room was silent and ice cold. She needed to open the windows so the soul could move on. Starting with Granny's, she opened them as far as they would go. Chicory covered all the mirrors in the house with blankets. Afterward, she crumbled to the floor. That's where Hawk found her hours later.

Everything was a blur of people flowing like water around an island, and that island was Chicory. A quiet immovable presence in the middle of all of the action. Watching, but not seeing a damn thing. She watched the mortician zip the bag over Granny's face, but it didn't feel real. How could she be gone?

The silence was deafening.

Days of folks checking in on her and giving her food she didn't eat. Did she sleep? She didn't know.

Etta dressed Chicory in the black dress like a life-sized doll. Where did this dress come from? The thought flitted across her mind before it was gone. The Preacher's lips moved but Chicory didn't hear a word. He looked familiar.

It wasn't until they were shoveling dirt over Granny's casket that Chicory said her first words in days. "Anyone have a jar?" Her voice was scratchy from lack of use. From out of nowhere an empty water bottle was shoved into her hands. She knelt at Granny's freshly dug grave and collected a few handfuls of earth. It's what she would have wanted.

In the following days Chicory ate because Hawk made her. Chicory was clean because Etta cleaned her. Chicory spoke because there were people she didn't know speaking to her about what was going to happen next.

"Give her some damn time to grieve," someone shouted. It sounded like Winter, though she'd never heard him angry. "She can live with us."

"She can't stay with y'all, a young girl like that … it ain't right," someone said. They're in a uniform. "There's a system in place … paperwork."

"I can stay right where I'm at," Chicory said from the chair she'd barely left. Hawk watched her warily.

The uniform was firm. "Actually you can't. You're only sixteen."

They just kept talking. The house was hers, but she couldn't have it until she was eighteen—whyever the hell that mattered. Her mother never put a father on her birth certificate, and she didn't have any known kin, so she was now a ward of the state. A ward until she turned eighteen, there's that number again, like it was magical.

She couldn't take much, a bag or two. But the trees wouldn't fit in there. The mountains wouldn't either. Neither Hawk. Nor Etta. Nor Emory. Not a damn thing that mattered at all.

Chicory flew out the door, leaving the shouting adults behind her. She ran straight up into the trees, hoping they'd swallow her whole.

Etta sobbed as she packed Chicory's bags, making sure she had what she needed in that way that Etta always took care of things that needed to be taken care of.

Hawk found Chicory lying on the rock beside their swimming hole. Either he knew that was where she'd be or there would always be an invisible string connecting them together. He hoped that was the case and he could follow that string and always find her. Hawk lowered his body to the ground next to hers and pressed all of himself to the back of her. His arms came around Chicory so tight maybe he could press them together and she could stay.

PART TWO

CHAPTER 12
AS I LIVE AND BREATHE

Every waking minute, Hawk saw those last fleeting moments. His hands cupping Chicory's face. "I love you. I will always love you. I will find you," he said over and over again trying to convince himself as well as her.

Emory crossed the pasture separating his family farm and Etta's trailer where she sat on the back step sobbing into the night. He carried his little beagle, Fern, over the fences with him. Em was feeling guilty he hadn't been there to say goodbye to Chic before they took her away. He would miss his friend. He also wished he had been there for Etta. But he was here now. Lowering himself onto the wooden step next to her, Emory put aside his awkwardness and took her in his arms. She soaked his shirt with her tears, as she cried and cried and cried. The little dog lay her head on Etta's lap like maybe she could offer some comfort too.

Chicory had gone more north and more east than she ever had before. For the first time in her life there wasn't a mountain in sight. So, by the time Winter filed the emergency custody paperwork and those papers finally had the right set of eyes on them, Chicory was gone. Long gone.

When his wife had died, Winter had a very young Hawk to keep him pushing through his days. Mindless tasks kept him too busy to think. After two weeks of grieving his friend, Winter made Hawk go back to school. At least it would keep him busy, anything was better than him lying in bed all day.

Hawk was no better than a Haint drifting along. Barely aware of his coming and going's. Then that prick Tommy opened his mouth, "Where'd your ugly girlfriend go?"

Hawk was barely aware he had punched Tommy in the face, until Tommy reciprocated by slamming his own fist into Hawk's mouth. Pain washed over him like ice-cold water, jolting him awake. His head snapped back from the force, blood spurted from his split lip, and he smiled. Hawk let out the rage and the frustration he had on Tommy, and Tommy didn't hold back. He gave as good as he got. It took three teachers to pull them apart.

Hawk stared at his reflection in the mirror. His broad face was a pummeled black and blue mess. A thick scab bisected his swollen lower lip. Good. At least now he looked as bad as he felt. He just needed to do one more thing. The hair Chicory loved hadn't been brushed or braided since she left. He couldn't bring himself to do it. There were still pale yellow strands of her own flowing tresses wrapped in his brush. A lingering piece of her reminding him she did exist. There was no artistry in what Hawk did next, he hacked away at his unkept locks with a pocketknife. It felt right.

Hawk stared at the school's Counselor with hostility from the uncomfortable chair in the man's office. He had been called in for an evaluation in "light of recent events."

Mr. Lee sighed. He had tried a few opening questions to get the young man in front of him to talk, though nothing penetrated the walls he had built. He would have to switch tactics.

"Remember Loretta?" the guidance counselor asked.

Hawk's jaws tensed so hard his teeth clacked.

"You know I'm helping her with her college scholarship applications," he added.

"Well, I guess then she'll be leaving too," Hawk mumbled.

"Hawk, just yesterday Etta cried in that very chair you're sitting in because she lost two friends when they took Chicory away. Do you understand? We know you're hurt and angry, but don't push everyone away."

Hawk jumped out of the chair; it screeched loudly with the force. He couldn't take it anymore. Yes, he'd been avoiding Etta. He couldn't look at her and not think of Chic. She was like salt in the already festering wound. He stomped to his locker before the next class. He slammed it shut and punched the metal in frustration. He was just so angry all the time.

When he turned Emory was blocking his way, his hackles raised at the ambush until Emory asked him, "You gonna fight me too?" Emory raised a golden eyebrow.

No. He could never hit Em, his heart was just as big as the rest of him. Sighing, Hawk turned and faced Etta, who he knew was standing right behind him. Her large blue eyes were just pouring tears.

"I lost Chicory too. The only person who knows how I feel is you and you're a selfish bastard," Etta sniffed. God, she was tired of crying. She thought by now she'd have dried up, but the tears just kept coming.

She was right. He was a selfish bastard. Hawk could only mumble what sounded like an apology and hug his friend.

Emory's big arms encircled them both, "group hug." If they weren't holding him up, Hawk may have crumbled with the overwhelming relief that they hadn't given up on him.

White. Off white. Cream.

"That's because studies show neutral colors do not evoke intense feelings." The woman with the clipboard says as she assessed the waif of a girl in front of her. Chicory didn't realize she had said the words aloud. "You need to eat, Chicory," the woman continued.

"The food here is terrible," Chicory croaked, her throat scratchy. She'd been practically mute since arriving. "I'm not hungry." She wasn't hungry. In fact, she felt nothing at all. It was as if she had died too. Her heart had been ripped out of her chest, her flesh stripped, and she stood there, nothing but a creaking skeleton, the bones picked clean. Wind whistled as it blew right through her. She was just so empty.

The woman prattled on ...

"As I live and breathe, I'll see you again someday," the voice mocked. Chicory was used to this person's chiding remarks. Roommate floated through the thick fog laying heavily in Chicory's mind. The words pierced the veil, as did the image on the front of the book. This ogre of a girl had been poking at Chicory since she arrived at the group home. Memories stirred as Chic beheld the cover, a corseted woman held in a passionate embrace.

Chicory made her roommate uncomfortable. She was too quiet and had weird, mismatched eyes.

"I thought this was from your girlfriend until I found these."
The roommate held up Chicory's sketchbook in her meaty
hands. Hawk looked out from the pages. Chicory had lovingly
rendered him in pencil. Pain lanced her heart. She'd let them
numb her so she wouldn't feel but she also let herself forget.

Moving faster than the roommate could react, Chicory
picked up a discarded pencil and pounced. She had faced real
monsters; this was just a bully. Chicory pushed the lead tip hard
enough that a trickle of blood glided down her roommate's
thick throat. The panicked eyes flickered back and forth in
terror, the pencil tip stabbed further in as she swallowed.

"What's the matter? Didn't mind poking bear, did you?
Didn't realize I had teeth?" Chicory mocked. "If you touch
my things again I'll rip your throat out while you sleep." The
roommate could only nod. Chicory let the other girl go and
leaned down to collect her books.

"Crazy bitch," the roommate muttered, but Chicory paid
her no mind.

She affectionately traced her finger across the inscription
Etta wrote. "As I live and breathe, I will see you again." And
Chic was still living, and she was breathing, and she would see
them again.

CHAPTER 13
BEGGARS CAN'T BE CHOOSERS

"You'll have to braid your hair and cover it when you're not at home," Ruth, Chicory's new Foster said from the front seat of the minivan. "We'll also give you appropriate clothes to wear."

"Yes, Ma'am," Chicory nodded in agreement from where she sat in the back of the van. She would agree to anything this stranger wanted because she was out. No more bars on windows.

Ruth and her husband John lived in the biggest house Chicory had ever been in. It had not one, but two sets of stairs, and sat smack dab between two other houses that looked just like it. In fact, the whole neighborhood was like that, and Chicory wondered how long it would take her to remember which one it was. Ruth's husband was a lazy middle class intellectual. No one knew exactly what he did for work, but he left at the same time every day in a uniform of khakis and a plain nondescript button up. Ruth had only one dream, and that was to be a stay-at-home mother and homemaker. After a few years of trying and no baby to show for it, it was sadly clear they had to look elsewhere than their own biology. Adoption was too expensive, John's salary was barely enough to support them alone, and the pair began their career in fostering.

Ruth and John kept six girls at all times, two to a bedroom. They typically took in girls a little older, not for anything untoward, older girls were just easier to take care of than the little ones.

Chicory was given a bland wardrobe of plain cotton tops and skirts in pale and pastel colors. Ruth explained it was their role as females to be meek and virtuous. They wore skirts to clearly define their gender, but they were never to show off their legs. It was their job to hinder any sinful thoughts that might cross the minds of their brothers in Christ. That didn't sound like Chicory's problem, but she knew when to keep her mouth shut. Besides, she had nowhere else to go. And even if she ran away, she didn't know how to get back to Dark Holler. She had somehow lost her way.

Church was on Wednesday evenings and all day on Sundays. Prayer was all week. Chicory wasn't a stranger to Jesus; in Appalachia he was one belief woven together with many others to make a big, beautiful rainbow quilt of spirituality. Ruth didn't believe anything else other than what her Church had to say was worth listening to, so Chicory didn't waste her breath. She had learned early on that Ruth had a funny way of deciphering scripture.

Ruth believed the Bible quite literally when it said "spare the rod spoil the child." Instead of thinking of it like a dousing rod leading to water, her interpretation was an actual beating. Ruth didn't understand the old ways and her and Chicory's first few weeks together were like a witch trial.

The first time Chicory had a switch taken to her; she had been caught pouring salt in the outside doorways. Chicory tried to explain it was to keep bad energy from entering the house, but Ruth wouldn't listen, she would not stand to have witchcraft in her home.

The second time, Chicory had been seen burying the hair she had cleaned from her brush. Again, pleading to her foster mother that she was only burying it so that the birds wouldn't take it back to their nests and drive her to madness. After that, Chicory learned she had to hide this part of herself away unless she wanted her backside to stay raw.

Chicory had been roomed with the youngest of her "sisters." Ruth called them "sisters," like she was housing a bunch of nuns, which in a way she was, since she was always preaching the importance of saving themselves for their future husbands. After weeks of being woken up by the girl, Chicory opened the covers of her own bed and coaxed the girl over. Her little body trembled as she snuggled into Chic's side. After a few minutes she relaxed into sleep. From that night on they settled into a routine.

The little girl was named Harleigh. She was eight years old and had found her mother dead in the hotel room they had been living in. Every night she saw her mother's lifeless eyes in her dreams. So, every night she crawled into Chicory's bed where Chicory would tell her stories in hopes they would give her something else to fall asleep to.

"Once upon a time there was an old woman in a forest, and she lived in a house made of gingerbread ... " Chicory began one night.

"I know this one. She tries to eat the children but they push her into the wood stove," Harleigh chimed in.

"No, you heathen, this is a different story. This old lady lives in a gingerbread house with a thousand cats," she laughed.

"That's not how it goes," the little girl giggled.

"In my story it does."

Night after night, Chicory found herself telling bedtime stories from the life she didn't want to forget, but she felt like it had been lived by someone else: Magic grannies that brewed potions from forest foliage to cure the sick, a boy who could turn into a bird and save a damsel in distress, a princess with ivory skin who lived in a castle with more brothers than she could count, a boy and his beloved dog who had the softest ears you've ever touched ... and even the tale of a girl who fought off a monster with just a rock. With these stories Chicory's heart healed a little and she was able to get a good night's sleep. She needed her wits about her, after the past few months of tutors and in-home classes (at the request of her case worker) she was going back to school.

CHAPTER 14
A BIRD IN THE HAND IS WORTH TWO IN THE BUSH

Etta sighed for the tenth time in minutes and replaced the book back on the shelf a little rougher than she should've. She had let her school counselor talk her into dual enrollment her senior year; between the extra classes and her part time job at the coffee shop, she was burning the candle at both ends. She had thought with her brothers being old enough to look after themselves she would have more freedom, but as she finished one assignment another needed to be turned in.

Emory leaned on the wall next to her. The sun streaked through the window, lighting him up like he was wearing a damn halo. He had a novel cradled in his hands, hands so big they engulfed the entire cover, completely obscuring it. Every gentle turn of the page set Etta's teeth grinding. She had thought by now she'd know what those hands felt like on her skin but no, he was a gentleman. A nice boy. Too damn nice. Etta huffs again in indignation, slamming another useless reference tome before returning it to the shelf. She couldn't concentrate, but this paper was due in just a few days.

It would be easier to work if Emory hadn't insisted on coming. They didn't see each other as much as they used to since both were busy setting up their futures after graduation. From where he leaned, Etta couldn't help sneak peeks at him. The last of childhood softness had left him with a chiseled jaw line, which he shaved every day to fight the beard that threatened to grow. The navy-blue shirt of his uniform stretched across his chest, the insignia of the fire station over his heart. As soon as he was of age, he had joined the department and somehow coaxed Hawk to join as well. Etta sniffed; she was sure anyone needing mouth to mouth wouldn't mind one bit when they saw those luscious lips coming at them. She growled and tried —but failed—to ignore Emory. He just took up so much space.

The long days volunteering had toned his body, while his summers interning at the park had left his skin bronzed. His sun-kissed hair matched the flecks of gold in his irises. Lord have mercy, she thought, he was so handsome. The problem was other girls thought so too. She wanted to smack him right in his beautiful face.

After another grunt Emory figured he should intervene on behalf of the library. She was abusing the written works.

"What's troubling you Loretta?" he asked. The use of her full name and the slight upturn of his mouth hinting that he probably knew exactly what was bothering her.

"Did Missy Herring ask you out today?" Etta blurted.

"Mmmhhhmmmmm," Emory replied, not looking up from his reading. He liked her flustered, it was recompense for her torturing him all these years.

"And?!" She exclaimed, hands gesturing in a "go-on" motion.

"And I politely declined." He closed his book with a thud while Etta visibly relaxed where she stood, a whole foot shorter than him.

"Careful, you wanted to wait until after graduation to date anyone—remember?—and this sounds an awful lot like jealousy," he teased. They had been toeing the line between friendship and more for a long time now. The lingering glances and overall hovering close enough to feel each other's body heat but not quite touching had racketed the sexual tension to the extreme. But he was going to wait as long as it took for Etta to make the first move.

"Because it is!" Etta screeched, shushing coming from the librarian elsewhere in the room. Etta had heard Missy telling her friend about it in English class and had never wanted to grab another girl by the hair and claw her eyes out so badly. Etta abandoned her work and stepped closer to Em. "You're mine." She poked him in the chest with a pink, nail-tipped finger.

"Is that so?" Emory challenged with a raised brow.

Her auburn hair was so thick the elastic band strained to hold it. Strands escaped the messy bun atop her head. Pink splotched her cheeks. She was absolutely stunning, even when she was furious.

Etta smashed her lips to his angrily. Their teeth clacked together.

"Ouch." Emory touched his mouth to make sure he wasn't bleeding. "That's … not what I expected," he laughed.

Etta tried to back away, embarrassed, but he grabbed her hip with one hand. "Is it my turn?" He asked huskily before cupping his other around her neck. Emory had been dreaming of their first kiss ever since he sat next to her in the cafeteria all those years ago. He feathered kisses along her jaw before reaching her soft lips.

"Oh my," Etta breathed out. Talking ceased as they deepened the kiss. Emory's fingers swept back and forth on the exposed skin on her side. That hand on her hip, the only thing keeping her from melting into a puddle right then and there on the floor. As they kissed between the shelves, in the ink and paper scented air, so sweetly, Etta thought she hadn't read anything as perfect as this. Nothing in her romance paperbacks had ever come close. It was like the scene had been written just for them.

Emory had no thoughts in his head. Just the rushing sound of his own blood as his heart pumped it through his body so fast it was dizzying.

The librarian turned around after almost walking in on their moment. She'd known those two for a quite a while now, and thought … it's about damn time.

CHAPTER 15
WHERE THERE'S BEES THERE'S HONEY

Beatrice Jones lived a charmed life. She had been raised by well-to-do parents who made sure their only child had opportunities they hadn't growing up. They had given Bea and her partner Gus the down payment for the land they turned into an urban farm oasis. In addition to growing herbs and vegetables to sell, the couple had also built three tiny houses on the property to house hired workers (who usually had nowhere else to go).

Bea didn't let her privilege go to waste. She looked at the world through rose-colored lenses and lived her life trying to make it a better place. Donations of fresh vegetables were always made to the local food pantry, the couple volunteered often within their community, and of course there was Bea's overwhelming softness for strays. The three tiny houses aside, there were two overweight pit bulls and a rooster that slept past sunrise roaming their farm. And at the moment, Bea touched her belly where one adopted frozen embryo had survived thawing and transfer, in hopes that she and Gus would be parents.

Not only did Bea's parents gift her with funds for the farm, but they also paid for the best education their money could buy. Masters in hand, Bea felt the best place to inspire others and influence young minds was at the local high school. It didn't take long for Bea to realize teenagers' minds were too occupied with social media and raging hormones to care about anything else. That didn't discourage her from trying to have deep discussions about incorrectly documented history and current world events. Surely, she could influence budding philanthropists to uphold the meaning of community and embrace the importance of helping others less fortunate. Try as she might, these kids' sense of self-importance was only exaggerated by helicopter parenting. They were all just biding their time before being admitted to their first choice of college that would likely cost as much as someone's whole yearly income.

At the start of the new school year, Bea, or Ms. Jones to these kids, did not expect any different. But then there *she* was, dressed like she had just come off the prairie and was about to churn butter at any moment. The girl was practically invisible in class but caught Bea's full attention by surprising her with an essay about why Columbus Day wasn't a holiday.

Curiosity brought Bea to the guidance office, where the counselor filled her in on a few details. Foster care. Great student. Loved art. But then Bea got "that feeling." It always started like a tickle in a place she couldn't reach to scratch. A thought that started as a wiggle but dug itself in until it constantly itched. She tried to convince herself that she was too busy to get involved, not to mention she didn't even know if the girl was in trouble and needed anyone concerning themselves with her life. But she couldn't stop herself from wondering, and in the end sometimes all you needed was a little nudge from the universe. (If you believed in all that stuff.) Which of course, Bea did.

Chicory scoffed loudly enough for her teacher to hear. Harleigh had been found by her grandmother and went off to live with her real family. It was great for the little girl, but she was now the latest name on a long list of losses for Chicory.

"What's the matter Chicory? You don't like my motivational poster?" Ms. Jones asked in regard to the whimsical paper by the desk: "No rain, no Flowers" spelled out in whirling floral letters.

Chicory replied, "Too much rain, you'll drown." How many more torrential downpours could she take? Every time she broke the surface to catch her breath another wave hit, dragging her under again. She turned to walk away but stopped and added, "Peppermint is good for morning sickness, but my Granny always recommended chive tea to expecting mothers." She said it in regard to the hot, steaming mug in her teacher's hands. Bea stared dumbfounded at the girl's back as she retreated. There was no way the girl would've known her condition. She was only a few weeks along.

This stayed with Bea the rest of the day and followed her home. There she found Gus in the living room laying on the couch with their two lazy dogs. He hated being still but was recovering from recent top surgery. The procedure was ill-timed with Bea's successful IVF, but they had waited almost an entire year for both and were at the mercy of their doctors' schedule. Sometimes life was just busier.

Gus was about to ask about her day when he saw the little dimple between her dark eyebrows. "What's up? I know that look."

"I was just thinking," she replied before setting her tote bag down and coming to rest on the floor next to him. "How are you feeling?" His cheeks looked a little rosy, so she placed a hand to his forehead.

"Don't distract me. I'm fine, but every time you get that look I have to do many hours of physical labor," he remarked.

His pale eyes sparkled with humor behind the round spectacles he wore.

Bea couldn't help the laugh that burst out. "That's not true." Even though it kind of was. Her thinking dimple had resulted in many of the structures on their property like the screened in building where they hosted communal meals. "Mostly ... but not all of the time." Subconsciously she splayed her hand over her abdomen. Gus smiled at his beautiful partner, despite the morning sickness, her brown skin practically glowed. His Bea, lover of the unloved. Not unlike himself, the teenage runaway Bea had met while serving meals at a homeless shelter. Together they had built a sanctuary for the unwanted and the lost.

"It's that student again ... I get the feeling she needs help." Then Bea explained why.

Chicory had told Ruth that she was staying after for tutoring, but instead, she was touring Ms. Jone's farm. (Chicory was still getting used to using the woman's first name.) They called it "Serendipity Farm." It even had a hand painted sign out front; each letter painted a color of the rainbow. Ms. Jones said they named their farm after all of the good surprises they've had from the universe. It sounded like some hippy bullshit to Chic, but then again, she was a little jaded with the universe at the time being. The main house sat at the front of the property; it reminded Chic so much like the house she grew up in it made her chest ache.

"How long before you turn eighteen?" Bea asked Chicory as they walked the paths between the raised gardens.

It wasn't quite spring yet, but Chicory could see how much they grew there. Trellises were built throughout, and perennial herb shrubs grew along the paths perfuming the air. The couple had made good use of their acres. "Somewhere between too soon and not soon enough."

"Chicory, you have an accent?" Gus asked. Chicory could not stop staring at her teacher's partner. He had short spikes of shockingly green hair, and his arms were covered in beautiful art. Plants and animals in stark black detail, Chicory was fascinated.

"I reckon to you I do," she laughed.

"Where are you from?" Bea asked curiously.

"A small mountain town in Appalachia." Chicory wondered if she'd ever lay her eyes on that town again.

"Do you know where you're going after graduation? Are you going back?" As Bea asked, Chicory's situation really looked desperate.

"Well, I don't know how far away the holler I grew up in is. I don't have a car or a license to drive one, and I don't even have two pennies to rub together. So, at the present I'm trying to figure it out." Chicory sighed. She knew all this in her heart but saying it out loud made it that much more depressing.

"Here's Cabin A. We just had a couple move on and it's currently available. The pay isn't much but it's what we can afford. We provide free housing and make plenty of meals to share. There's electricity but no running water. That building in the middle of everything is a shower house." Bea pointed to a structure painted with sunflowers all over the sides before continuing, "If you don't have a lot of knowledge about gardening don't worry, we'll show you the ropes." She opened the cabin's door, which was painted none other than sky-blue.

Serendipity indeed. Chicory couldn't help but think. "I helped tend a garden as long as I can remember right up until recently." She hadn't had a fresh vegetable in a coon's age. The group home and her foster home only served canned.

"What do you think? I know you've got a great opportunity to start at the local community college with grants. You could easily work here while you go to school." It wasn't just the fact that Chicory really had nowhere else to go, it was the open sincerity on Bea's face that did it. Not to mention, it sounded like an actual plan to someone who was in the process of trying to make one.

She didn't have much to pack, just the same bag she'd been dragging around, her sketchbooks and the much-loved novel from Etta still hidden there. After offering to not tell her caseworker about the relocation so Ruth could get Chicory's last few checks, there wasn't much of a fight to make her stay.

It would be the first time Chicory had been alone in a long, long time. Though that didn't keep her from being lonely.

Chicory looked around the one-room cabin. A full-size bed dressed in fresh linens was pushed in the far left corner with a lamp on a nightstand beside it. In the other corner stood a tall wardrobe for a closet, and there was a table at the window. There was a small kitchenette to the right of the door that consisted of a hot plate, microwave and a mini fridge. After Chicory put her belongings away, she started cleansing the space by emptying the saltshaker in the open windowsill and doorway. Gus walked by with the two dogs at his heels. He saw her, just waved and yelled, "Let me know if you need anything," before continuing down the path. Chicory smiled and let herself hope.

CHAPTER 16
WHAT CAN'T BE CURED MUST BE ENDURED

Hope is waiting for the happy ever after. It's the optimistic outcome, fully manifested. As graduation came and went and the trees changed from green to jewel tones, Hawk had finally lost hope. He found himself in a desolate place. He felt barren, like winter trees.

Feeling downhearted was made far worse when his two best friends were so in love it made him actually sick. Oftentimes, Hawk couldn't even stand to be around Etta and Em, which was awful because they were the best people he knew and didn't deserve the ugly thoughts in his head.

Young adulthood threatened boredom most days. His peers were buying houses and furnishings and settling into domesticity at an alarming rate. None of them had yet had their hopes and dreams crushed by reality. Hawk typically zoned out when anyone talked about the future. He really couldn't care less.

During the day, Hawk kept busy by working with his dad. The work was physically demanding, but he got paid to climb trees and play with a chainsaw. As for a job, it didn't get much better than that. On nights and weekends, he ran calls with EMS. Nothing dampened a pity party faster than seeing folks worse off than himself. Hawk's heart may have been broken but it was still ticking. When he couldn't keep himself too busy to think, he thought about ways to forget. *Narcan* enough people, and you understand that some types of escape you never come back from. So, when the Chicory sized void threatened to swallow him, he'd settle for just a cold beer or two.

Emory was in another state at Park Law Enforcement training. Etta was busy with school and brothers.

Unwillingly, Hawk found himself even lonelier than usual. That being said, it didn't take much convincing to get him to join a few of the other guys from the station for a bonfire. They were having it in some local field. Ironically, the guys liked making fires just as much as putting fires out and it didn't take long to set a giant blaze. Sullen, Hawk huddled in a folding chair nursing his drink. Under the clear night sky, he found himself begin to relax. His body grew warm with the heat of the fire and the alcohol in his bloodstream. His head was getting fuzzy and blessedly started emptying of thoughts.

A moment later he saw her, lit by the bonfire's amber glow. She undulated her hips in a way that you wouldn't think you could to country music. Her hair was dark and straight, and she didn't remind him of anyone at all. The dancer's doe eyes watched him back and then she surprised the hell out him by curling one finger in a "come hither" gesture. Hawk surprised himself even more by getting to his feet and following her. They danced a few songs together, if you'd call their sensual writhing dancing, before she tugged him to a dark corner of the field. Thankfully she didn't notice his shaking hands as they fumbled with inexperience. Sheltered behind brush, this magical creature took the lead, and in the lustful haze Hawk forgot to be sad.

CHAPTER 17
YOU CAN'T MAKE A SILK PURSE OUT OF A SOWS EAR

Etta put away the last of the dishes from breakfast. She'd have to get moving if she planned on being punctual to class. Her teachers had all been pretty lenient with her situation being as it was. A situation she was utterly sick and tired of. Etta filled the tray with enough food to get her bed ridden momma through the day. Etta's teeth ground tightly at the thought. "She's bedridden by her own damn choice!" Resentment had taken the space in Etta's heart where love and familial duty had been, leaving a bitter taste in her mouth.

Guiltily, she tried to remember times before, but those memories were tainted by the present. Bathing her momma, clipping her toenails and even changing her pads had started to make Etta disgusted and hateful. Her lower back constantly ached from stress and the increasing difficulties of taking care of someone who had let herself get morbidly obese. Any moment, Etta was going to break.

Etta glanced at the healthy options she had put on the tray, though the effort was wasted. Her momma would wait until she was gone and call the local sub shop, Somehow she had convinced the driver to deliver the food right to her bedside. Momma would then hide the trash until the smell gave her away and the two women would fight like hell. Jolene arguing

Etta didn't feed her enough and Etta arguing they didn't have the money to spend on all the carry out. It was embarrassing, especially when Em's parents had gone ahead and bought the boys their last pairs of shoes.

Those boys worshipped both Emory's. It took one tractor ride for Emory Sr. to have the youngest three as farm hands, help that was desperately needed with Em away for training. They stayed next door more than they did home. Etta couldn't blame them; she could rarely stand to be there anymore herself. As the boys got bigger the trailer got smaller and smaller, and the walls felt like they were going to cave right in.

The drive to school took about an hour. Thanks to Emory's dad, who not only taught her how to drive, but helped her buy the cute wagon she had to get there. The man had hemmed and hawed over the motor, run his hands over the tires, checking treads and pumping the brakes repeatedly, before he deemed it fit for her.

Taking a moment to calm her nerves, Etta braced herself to enter her momma's bedroom.

Jolene knew her daughter would come in to check on her before she left so she didn't bother to call her in. She had one more thing left to do and then she'd be ready.

Setting the tray down on the bedside stand, Etta asked, "You need anything before I go, Momma?"

"Have a minute to sit a spell?" Jolene asked and patted the bed, her bed that had become a floral duvet-covered prison.

"Yes, ma'am," Etta replied, before asking, "What is it? You feeling alright?" Her big blue eyes scanned her momma's body checking for anything amiss.

Truth be told, Jolene hadn't felt alright in a long, long time, but she had been thinking clearly, lately. Clearly enough to make a plan. She asked, "Can you take my oxygen tank to get refilled today?"

"Why'd you let it get so low?" her daughter chided.

"I'll be fine one day without it, you hen pecker," Jo laughed.

"You have all your meds?" Etta inquired, knowing she'd already gotten them this week, but there were so many lined up along the nightstand, forgetting one was easy. Those bottles were the only things keeping her momma alive these days.

"They're all here thanks to you." Jolene paused. "Loretta," her solemn tone caused her daughter to face her fully, brows furrowed. "I'm so proud of you. You are the best decision I ever made."

Etta went to speak but her momma cut her off. "My daddy was a preacher. Your daddy was in his congregation. His daughter was my best friend. I remember how it hurt, but he was the first person to tell me I was beautiful. Being big, you get called a lot of things, but beautiful?" She laughed sarcastically. "By the time I understood I was with child, it was too late, he just handed me five hundred dollars and dropped me off at a clinic in a place I had never been. A city. I had never seen a city before." Sadness flowed from Etta, her heart breaking for the young girl her momma had been. "They gave me a free exam and even a sonogram. They told me I was having a little girl, that was you, Etta ... They would have helped me find a nice family to raise you if I wanted. I asked to think about it and thanked them. I sat on the bench outside and watched the city move. All the while I held the printout with your shape on it in my hand, and kept tracing your face with my finger. I could already see you were perfect. When I went to put the sonogram into my backpack there was money stuffed in the front pouch. Ones and fives all crinkled up. It must have been from the collection plate. There was a note in there, in my momma's handwriting, it said, 'I tried my best … ' That's all we can do as parents is try our best and hope it's enough. I walked to the nearest bus stop and rode it until the last stop. Then I got on another and another and did the same until I came to a town with cute brick buildings, and the mountains so close, they looked like if they fell over, they'd crush it. I stopped in a café, the one you work in actually, and used the bathroom. There on the community board was a paper with a trailer for rent. It was hard, but we made it work, didn't we? I've done a lot of things I regret, too many to count. But choosing you is not one of them." With that she kissed her daughter's head, which had come to rest on her chest while she told her story. "All right, go on and git before you're too late."

Tearfully, Etta nodded, got up and grabbed the empty oxygen tank.

"Close the door on the way out would you, please?"

This was odd, but Etta was too lost in her own thoughts to pay it any attention. "Love you momma."

What Jolene didn't mention in her story was that her daddy wasn't just a preacher, he was also a burn talker. He passed it to her just as his momma did to him and her daddy to her. Generation after generation. Man to woman to man. Jo had taught her second youngest son, but he couldn't tell a soul because if he did his gift would be lost.

She lit the candle that sat amongst the pill bottles, running her hand through the flame and feeling no heat. She found the bottle she was looking for and emptied it into her palm, then began to swallow the pills one after the other. Jo then picked up the candle and held the flame to her bed. The fire licked along the bedspread before she let the candle fall to the floor where the old dry carpet caught fast. Jo lay back against her pillows, her eyelids already heavy, and began to recite the prayer to take the heat out of a burn.

"When you pass through the waters, I shall be with you; and through the rivers, they shall not overwhelm you; when you walk through fire you shall not be burned, and the flame shall not consume you."

By the time she finished the last words of the verse, Jolene's heart had stopped beating, and the flames engulfed her whole—she didn't feel a thing.

Mrs. Green was giving the potted plants on her porch a hearty drink from the watering can. An odd feeling settled on her shoulders like a tap, it made her look toward the trailer park that sat just beyond their pasture. "Emory!" she screamed.

Home for a long weekend, and catching up on rest, Emory was still barefoot and dressed in his sleep clothes. When he finally made his way to the porch, his mom asked, "Is that smoke?" She'd barely finished her question before Emory was running as fast as he could toward Etta's home. Watering can forgotten, Mrs. Green dashed inside to call for help.

Emory's training kicked in as he ran around the double-wide. The boys were at school, he assured himself. So was Etta. Her car was gone, confirming this. Smoke was curling from the D side, Jolene's bedroom. There was no way she could leave without help. With dread, he realized she must still be inside.

The front door wasn't hot to the touch and blessedly unlocked. He yelled, "Anyone inside!" After opening it and receiving no answer. He saw flames climbing the walls and black and gray smoke billowing from under the main bedroom door, obstructing any rescue. He was barefoot, for God's sake, and if he rushed into that blazing room, the arriving squad would have two victims to save. Sirens wailed louder and louder as the Cavalry approached. Battalion Chief was first to jump off the fire engine. Emory shared his assessment while two other crew members readied the line. Another engine, a tanker and an ambulance, arrived for backup. The scene was loud, but all Emory could hear was the beating of his own heart.

Minutes were all that passed as the fire steadily consumed the flimsy material that had been used to construct the mobile home. Moments later, the whole right side of the structure collapsed. Emory stood back and watched as gallon after gallon of water was pumped out of the tanker, but in the end, Etta's childhood home was reduced to smoldering remains. And somewhere in the rubble they found what was left of Etta's mother.

"Why didn't you call me?!" Etta screamed as she pounded Emory's chest with her fists. "Why, Em?" she pleaded.

"I didn't want you driving a wreck ... I did it to keep you safe." He caught her as the fight went out of her body and she crumbled toward the ground.

Etta stared at the leftover fragments of her life. From one moment to the next ... gone. Guilt and grief warred over which were going to make her feel worse. Hadn't she wished for an escape—mere hours earlier? But now the weight of sadness settled over her, she'd never be able to go home again. And her poor momma ...

Her Momma. Realization hit her hard like a slap. Her momma had so much taken from her already, in the end she didn't want the last of her self respect to be taken, too. It would have been the talk of the town, trying to move her body, not if, but when she died. Etta hoped her momma had finally found some peace.

"What now?" Etta asked Emory as they sat on his family's front porch. They watched as the sun set over the corpse of the double wide, putting an end to this long traumatic day.

"Well, mom and dad are helping the boys get settled in the two extra bedrooms and I guess you'll just have to sleep in mine until we save enough money to buy your dream home," he replied frankly.

"A house before a ring? How millennial of you, Emory Green," she joked, until guilt pierced her chest and her smile faltered. How could she joke and smile after today?

"We both know you'd take a house over a ring any day," he squeezed her knee where it rested against his.

He knew her so well. Well ... maybe he didn't know everything. After a pause she admitted softly, "Em, I don't want any kids. I'm too sick of taking care of other people. Is that selfish?"

"Not at all. I think you're due for a little selfishness. I'll take care of you," he answered honestly. "Besides, you'd be the one having them, so I think that gives you more say than me." Fern poked her little head between them. Emory scratched her ears how she liked, and she crawled into his lap. "But if you say no dogs, that could be a deal breaker."

Just as Etta was about to answer, a truck came flying through the graveled trailer park. Even from the porch they could tell from the shape of the silhouette, it was Hawk that jumped out of the vehicle's driver side and ran around the property, surveying the damage. After his inspection he vaulted over the pasture fence and raced up the hill towards them. He cleared the second fence before coming to a stop before the couple.

Breathless, he said, "I got here as fast as I could. I was working two counties away." Hawk paced in front of them, "Shit, Etta. Are you ok? No, of course you aren't." His dark hair was sticking straight up from running his fingers through it anxiously. "I'm so sorry about your mom. Fuck!" He was a tornado of chaotic energy, hotheaded to a fault, but sometimes he said it best. Hawk flopped his body on Etta's other side, then wrapped his arm behind her back and set his hand on Emory's shoulder. Em returned the gesture and the three sat like that until the black, starless night settled completely around them.

CHAPTER 18
FAR TO MIDDLIN'

The first year at Serendipity was a blur. By losing herself in the muscle memory of farm tasks, Chicory found her way. Graduation came and went with little fanfare. (Just how she wanted.)

If Bea and Gus hadn't helped Chicory transition into adulthood, the transition probably wouldn't have been so smooth. Between readying themselves for the arrival of their own child, they treated Chicory like she was theirs as well. The couple gave her driving lessons, got her an age-appropriate wardrobe, helped her set up a bank account, and even step into the modern world with her very own cell phone.

Bea explained social media to Chic, telling her she may be able to find her old friends. But the thought of seeing them going on without her was too much, so like a coward she didn't even try. For the first time since leaving the Holler, she couldn't remember her address, but Chicory looked up her old school in GPS. Four hours and eleven minutes. It might as well have been on the other side of the country since she couldn't drive or have a car. She was learning though. One day at a time.

Azure was born just as the fall crops were being harvested and Chicory had stopped blushing every time the figure model took off their robe in drawing class. As soon as she laid eyes on that baby it was love at first sight. She took every chance she got to get him from his weary parents. They didn't mind one bit.

Holidays were celebrated. Chicory strung garland she made from dried oranges and twine in her tiny abode. She made candy from potatoes, sugar and peanut butter. The memory came unbidden from the recesses of her mind, of making the holiday treat with her Granny. The longest night of the year didn't seem so dark, Chicory was practically luminescent with happiness.

The cabin tenants rotated with the seasons, typically moving on when the cold air blew in. Sometimes Chicory didn't even have time to remember their names before they moved on. Azure learned to walk as another year slipped through Chicory's fingers, holding onto time was like trying to catch falling rain.

Spring brought new faces, which were welcome with the impending growing season. Chicory and Gus had the seeds started in the greenhouse. Though in just a few weeks business would be booming with not only crop care, but farmer's markets and onsite sales. A couple everyone called the Erins moved into Cabin C. And a young man named Xavier took up residence in Cabin B.

Chicory preferred actual labor to sales, so she often found herself companionably working with Xavier. In the beginning their interactions mostly consisted of "good mornings" or "how are you's." Then after a while graduated to full blown conversations, Xavier talking enough for the both of them. He laughed loud and often, and his teeth shone bright white in his raw umber colored skin. His genial personality, aesthetically pleasing exterior and the way his long deft fingers handled the plants with care had nothing to do with Chicory's preference to work alongside him. No, it was because the Erin's fought all the time. At least this is what she told herself.

After much prodding, Xavier found out Chic had spent some time "in the system." He had no idea how, after everything, she'd stayed so gentle, though it suited her. Warm days Chicory gardened barefoot, wore her hair in long braids and carried a satchel across her back. She never failed to have something you'd need in that seemingly bottomless bag. The other workers gave her wide berth, claiming they found her strange. Chicory certainly had some strange ways, Xavier found he liked them. She was definitely full of surprises.

On the day Chicory got her driver's license Xavier picked her up and swung her around. Then asked, "what are you going to do to celebrate?"

Chicory replied with the biggest grin, "I want a tattoo." She'd been obsessed with Gus' since the first day they'd met. After the first design, she got another. And another. Then a thin gold hoop through her septum and more gold hoops up both her ears. All that time adrift had taught Chicory she would indeed find herself again, that didn't mean she was the same. It just made sense to express that on the outside. She was permanently changed, now her body was too.

This winter Xavier and the Erin's didn't leave, they all found jobs in the city to work part time until the next growing season. Xavier was waiting tables at a restaurant and often brought desserts back home with him. He also brought home women as well. Chicory felt a longing she didn't understand and wondered what that was like, going home with someone, but none of them stayed long enough for her to ask.

Xavier was an ass man, a breast man, hell any-divine-feminine-curve man. All of the above Chicory did not have, and yet her beauty snuck up on him. Her kind of beauty crept through the cracks in the walls he'd built up for his own protection. She was slight and long limbed and moved through the world with whimsy. Shades of dusky pink shone through her freckled skin, her two-toned eyes and her hair that hung down in golden waves to her waist made for something otherworldly. Xavier wouldn't have been surprised to see gossamer wings tucked behind her back, Faerie Queen that she was. He could understand how mortals were content to dance to their deaths, he'd surely made a habit of doing whatever she asked.

"Chicory, why in the hell are we planting potatoes in the middle of the night?" He asked from deep inside the hood of his sweatshirt. When she'd asked him to meet her tonight, this was not what he had in mind. "I'm freezing my ass off."

"You plant potatoes at night because the light hurts their eyes," she answered seriously.

"Chicory, you've said some weird shit, but I think this takes the cake." He laughed at his friend's angry look. "Okay, but make it fast. I'm scared of the dark."

She answered from where she was kneeling next to the upturned earth, "There's nothing to be afraid of, I put railroad spikes in each corner of the property." She pointed north, south, east and west.

"I'm not even going to ask why ... but where did you come across railroad spikes?" He bent down to put the potato spuds in the holes she had dug.

"The train tracks. Where else?" she replied incredulously.

He glanced over at her. "Chicory!" He gasped and clutched his chest sarcastically. "Did you steal?" He barely finished before bursting into a fit of giggles.

"No, you smart ass, I walked the tracks until I found ones that had come loose. If you'd plant as fast as you talked, we'd be done a hell of a lot faster," she huffed. Xavier just laughed harder.

Something had gone around the farm, laying everyone low except Chic. After a full twenty-four hours without Xavier leaving his cabin, Chicory took it upon herself to barge on in. He lay in a cocoon of comforters in the middle of his bed. Chicory opened the window.

"What are you doing? It's freezing!" Xavier mumbled from his fetal position, wrapped in blankets.

"You gotta let the sick out," she explained. Next, she pulled back his blankets despite his protests and placed a soppy wet dish towel on his bare chest.

The smell was so strong Xavier gagged. "Oh I see, you're putting me out of my misery," he said dramatically before trying to remove the offensive bundle.

"Leave it. It will break up the congestion in your chest. It's just an onion paste." Chicory poured something hot and steamy from a thermos she had carried in. "Drink this," she demanded, and placed a mug in his hands.

Xavier couldn't smell what it was because of the offensive stench of the chest compress. "It tastes like bog water," he grimaced.

"Good, that means it's strong and will thicken your blood." She nodded and checked his fevered brow one more time before she finished her fussing and left. Xavier couldn't remember a time when anyone had fussed over him at all.

There was a deep sink outside the bath house that was used for scrubbing up after a day in the dirt. Xavier and Chicory had just finished putting hundreds of tomato plants in the ground. Xavier hissed in pain as he worked the soap's lather over a wart he could not get rid of.

Chicory noticed and held out her small hand for his much larger one. "Let me see." She turned his hand one way then the other, inspecting the lump, before nodding to herself. After rummaging through that satchel of hers, she pulled out a case of sewing needles. "Just trust me," she said after he noticeably winced.

Chicory pierced the needle into the wart, then dug a hole under the sink, out of anyone's way, and buried the needle. Xavier just watched the strange ritual. He'd say it was the weirdest thing he'd ever seen but they'd been friends for long enough now that it wasn't. He'd learned when it came to this girl, just trust the process. Chic wiped away the blood from the needle's prick and applied a poultice she'd also procured from her bag. After wrapping the small wound with gauze, she said, "That should do it." The next morning when he took the wrapping off his finger, he wasn't even shocked the wart was gone.

"Is Chicory a witch?" Xavier asked Bea and Gus. He'd caught them outside, drinking their morning coffee, watching Azure ride his tricycle. His bosses, who had become his friends over the months he'd lived on their farm, shared a look before answering.

"Chicory would never call herself that, but she grew up with her Gran who taught her the old ways," Bea told Xavier. "Ways that seem odd to us but have been passed on for generations. I don't know if that makes her a witch, but Chicory is magical and very important to me ... you understand?" It was perfectly clear to Xavier that he'd be out on his ass if he answered this incorrectly. Gus nodded in agreement.

"It's not what you think," Xavier held his hands out in defense. "She just has cured me a few times ... that's all. I like Chic." He asked because he wanted to know what kind of spell she'd put on him. He liked Chic alright, a little too much.

"You haven't had any sleepovers lately," Chicory commented as they pulled weeds. She didn't want to bring it up, but like a damn fool she couldn't help herself.

"Why? You worried about my sleeping habits?" he teased. Her cheeks colored to the shade of a rose petal. He loved to tease her just so he could see her blush.

"I keep track so I know if I'll be running into any strangers in the bathroom come morning. Don't want to scare the bejesus out of anyone," she lied.

No, he hadn't brought anyone home in a long time because it seemed his type had changed from voluptuous promiscuous vixen to forest pixie. Specifically, the one in front of him. "Thank you for reminding me how lonely I am. That reminds me, my favorite comic book has been made into a movie, and I have no one to go with. Please, Chic don't make me go alone," he pleaded, and made a ridiculous pouty face.

"I've never been to a movie theater before," she replied.

"What?! It's settled then. Tonight, we'll go tonight!" He whooped excitedly and jumped up.

Chicory's stomach was a mess of butterflies. She hoped she wouldn't puke.

Xavier knew he should be watching the big screen, however when the action got going Chicory grabbed his wrist and held on, her face a kaleidoscope of emotions. She gasped. She cried. Had he ever felt that strongly in his entire life? "What did you think?" He asked her softly. The credits were running, the theater was emptying, and he was enraptured by the tears streaking down her face. Her impossibly long lashes clumped together in wet spikes. He ran his thumb over her cheek to catch a wayward tear.

"It was almost too much," she answered, and he wholeheartedly agreed.

Bea, Gus and Chicory sat in the grass while Azure pushed a plastic dump truck filled with miniature dinosaurs between them. Chicory paid no mind to the child as she watched Xavier carry boxes of produce to an awaiting box truck. She should get up and help but sweat shone on his dark skin like glitter and she was enjoying the view.

Bea followed her friend's hungry gaze and couldn't help but smile. "Chicory," she began gently. "I know you've been busting your ass towards your end goals, but you can enjoy the journey getting there in the meantime. You picking up what I'm putting down?" Bea raised a brow and pointedly looked from Chicory to Xavier. With the pink spreading across her face, she couldn't deny she knew exactly what her dear friend was saying, and she couldn't deny she'd been thinking the exact same thing.

Chicory knew she was acting off; she couldn't help it. How did one do this? Xavier definitely noticed how tense she'd been and as they were washing dishes after dinner in the main house, he came right out and asked, "What's up with you?"

Chicory's heart was beating as fast as a hummingbird's. "I'm fine. What are you doing tonight?" she spit out.

"I'm not planting shit in the middle of the night with you if that's what you're asking," he said smugly while drying a plate.

"Do you want to come over tonight ... to my cabin?" The question was out so fast. She panicked a little. She couldn't take it back.

Shocked, Xavier dropped the plate in his hand. But he nodded as he cleaned up the shards. For once in his life, he was speechless.

The walk over to Cabin A had been silent and awkward. Chicory leaned on the door as Xavier looked though her little space. Herbs hung to dry, drawings were displayed on the walls and it was so perfectly her, he smiled. After his quick perusal, he turned to face her. "Okay, Chicory, I'm here. What do you want to do now?"

Who moved first, they never knew. They came together with the force of two people who'd been denying themselves of each other for way too long. A tangled mess of limbs, lips and tongues. Chicory ripped off his shirt. Skin, she needed to feel his skin. He gasped as she ran her hands along his torso. Their kiss broke long enough for him to pull her top off, too. He barely had time to hold onto her thighs as she jumped to wrap her legs around his waist. He turned them to lower her down on the mattress, his weight pushed her deliciously down. "Chicory," he was breathless as he said her name. "You're one of the best friends I have ever had. I'm no good with hearts ... don't trust me with yours."

Fingers entwined; this was a moment of honesty. "I don't have one to give, what about my body ... ." Her voice was so husky she hardly recognized it.

"That I know how to treat well." His dark chuckle set her body on fire just as much as the feeling of her pants and panties as he slid them off her. He paused as she lay bare before him, hair spread over the pillow, dressed in nothing but the sliver of moonlight from the cabin's window. For all his talk about hearts it never occurred to him to consider his own.

"I've never done this before," Chicory whispered.

Of course she hadn't. "We'll start slow. We don't have to do everything tonight," Xavier said. But Chicory had waited long enough, and everything was what she wanted. So in the end that is what he gave her. Xavier gave her his all.

CHAPTER 19
PUT YOUR MONEY WHERE YOUR MOUTH IS

First, he earned Eagle Scout. The following years he spent volunteering with the fire department, training as a paramedic, and joining Search and Rescue. He spent his summers attending and then supervising the Youth Conservation Corps. Certification after certification. Then countless thirteen-dollar hours in the admission booths collecting entrance fees and providing trail information, where he intentionally directed hikers away from certain locations.

Everything had been worth it, Emory reminisced as he picked Fern up and set her in the state issued pickup truck, the words "Park Officer" emblazoned on the side. The only thing on his body more meaningful than his badge was the titanium band encircling the ring finger of his left hand.

The sky was blackening with ominous clouds, the telltale sign a storm was moving in. He hoped most of the hikers out there had enough sense to high tail it out down off the mountain, but he had been in his position long enough now to know that wasn't always the case. Folks loved taking risks. Hadn't he, before he knew any better?

Doing emergency work, Emory was no stranger to death. However, coming up on an emergency scene and seeing tragedy was one thing, finding a dead body among the serene beauty of the outdoors was another thing entirely. His first macabre discovery was at the bottom of a waterfall. The victim had apparently slipped from above and fallen the dozens of feet into the water below. In the following months, he'd seen suicides, auto accidents and participated in dozens of trail rescues, which didn't always mean the lost were found. Emory hadn't anticipated as much action. He wasn't complaining, but it did make him appreciate the boring days.

Emory hadn't run into any Moon-Eyed People since his ill-advised monster hunting. No Not Deer either. Though he'd be lying if he said he hadn't experienced some unexplainable occurrences. There was definitely something that liked to tease him by calling his name when he worked overnight shifts. When whatever-it-was called out to him, it reminded Emory of this parrot his great aunt had, the way human words came out of a mouth they weren't made for. Naturally, he'd ignored it.

Emory's hopes for an uneventful night we're dashed to bits when an emergency call came in at nine. Three girls hadn't come back from a planned day hike. Sure enough, he found their vehicle parked in the lot at the trail head. By now the wind had picked up, but fingers crossed, the rain would hold off a little while longer. The words were barely out of his mouth when the sky opened up. With the downpour there would be fewer options for rescue, either way, it looked like it was going to be a long night.

The small building that housed the ranger's office was full of gathered volunteers. The weather inhibited any air support, but amongst the group, there were a dozen trained well enough to go in on foot. They had to go in tonight. These girls would be facing exposure, predators and ... other things lurking out there.

Unsurprisingly, Hawk was there, but Emory was shocked to see Tommy amongst the participants. Emory did not know if his old friend had much hiking experience, but his little sister was one of the girls out there. Tommy insisted on being included.

Map spread before them all, Tommy pointed to the area his sister's last text said they'd made it to. Luckily the girl was smart enough to share her itinerary with her brother.

The volunteers would start on the same path, then at the mile and a half marker, split into two groups where the trail forked. Hawk and Emory shared a look. It had been many years since they'd taken that trail; one way would take them to an overlook, the other to a waterfall. "Let's hope we find them before anything else up there does," Emory thought to himself, but by the look on Hawk's face it was clear they were thinking the same damn thing.

"What do we do if ... " Hawk said low enough for only Emory to hear.

"I hope it doesn't come to that, but a few of us have firearms just in case," Emory winced.

Fern whined when Emory shut her in his office, the weather was too bad for canine help. He loaded up his rescue pack, secured his harnesses and ropes, and made sure the group had enough litters to carry out the exhausted or injured. He sent a quick text to Etta, and out into the stormy night he went.

The headlamps on their helmets barely made a difference in the wood's darkness. Rain thundered atop the canopy, at least the dense trees kept the water from pelting them directly. The wet trail was hard to navigate, it took over an hour to get to the split.

Water flowed down the switchbacks from the storm's runoff. "These are gonna be hell getting down," Tommy said behind him. Emory agreed but just concentrated getting up slick rocks, his boots sinking in the mud with every step.

Just as their smaller group reached the top of the mountain trail, where the path became flat for a brief reprieve, a scream penetrated the rain's uproar. The rescuers hurried their pursuit.

"What the fuck is that?!"

Emory's headlamp beam swung jerkily as he assessed the scene. They found the girls huddled together under a shallow rock overhang escaping the storm. Thankfully the weather was free of lightning, or they'd have been in the worst possible place.

About ten feet from the hunkered girls stood a creature illuminated in the group's collected lamp light. Emory's body froze as he and this thing before him regarded each other. It was pale, but way too big to be one of the Moon-Eyed People. Also, the thing's head was completely hairless. The creature hunched over on all fours, but it was obvious if this beast stood up on two legs, it would tower over them all.

"Jesus Christ," someone muttered behind him.

"No, not Jesus," Emory thought, as he stared at the eyes, well, the absence of eyes. In the monster's head were two holes, completely void of anything but absolute emptiness. The mouth, just a horizontal rip in the bottom of the thing's head.

Emory stood there for minutes, or hours, he couldn't really tell, until the acrid smell of someone losing their bladder woke him from the creature's trance.

"Don't shoot! There are rocks everywhere here. Ricochet ... " Emory yelled half truthfully. Em didn't know why, but somehow, he knew this was the creature that played with him on night duty shifts. Somehow, he couldn't bear to see it shot down. Lord forgive him, but it made no difference to him what the creature had planned for these girls.

Seeming to understand their truce, the thing nodded its bulbous head before slinking away into the trees, impossibly silent.

As soon as it was gone, the group sprang into action.

"Tommy!" his sister cried as her brother took hold of her in a tight embrace.

"What happened? Lose the trail in the rain?" Emory asked. "Anyone hurt?"

One of the girls answered, flinching as Hawk checked her injury. "I slipped coming down the scramble on the other side and hurt my ankle, it's been slow going to get back, and then the storm hit us."

Despite trying to escape the elements the girls were soaked, shivering, and in danger of hyperthermia.

Warming blankets were wrapped around them, and they were loaded onto the litters. Two by two the group slowly carried them out.

The hike turned into a slide on the steeper areas of the trail, with the crew sitting on their rears and guiding the litters down from one solid point to the next, or even passing them along, bucket brigade style. At times they had to leave the trail and take the steeper, rockier, hillside where the switchback would have been too treacherous or slippery. The rain pummeled down relentlessly. Their minds protected them from the horrendous thing they had seen, and Emory could hear bits of their conversation, trying to make jokes, or to make sense of the nonsensical. "That thing back there ... just a hallucination ... maybe a sick bear ... an albino bear? ... maybe some crazy dude ... in a costume? ... did you see how tall it was? ... no ... did you see the way it looked at Em? ... ya'll are just stressed ... did we call support yet? ... "

By the time the group made it safely back with the found girls, the sun had started to rise, the sky was dusky blue, and the rain had finally stopped.

"Any idea what that really was back there?" Hawk asked once they've handed the girls off to waiting paramedics. If anyone had an idea, it'd be his monster loving friend. Hawk was too tired to have nightmares about it, besides he'd seen far worse.

Emory scratched his stubbled chin. Embarrassingly, he had thought of nothing else on the group's descent.

"I think we just met a Crawler." He looked at Hawk, completely sincere when he answered. He wondered how many of those things were out there. How long have they lived in these mountains? Where did it crawl out from? The underbelly of the oldest rocks in the world?

What would Emory put in his report? 'Unknown male harassing three girls ... ran off when approached ... rescue prioritized?'

Hawk considered his friend; they had bruise-colored matching circles under both of their eyes from the long night. Yawning, he answered, "Huh. Ain't that some shit?" Then clapped his friend on the back, "Let's hit the diner. I'm about starved." And that was that.

CHAPTER 20
CAN'T SEE THE FOREST FOR THE TREES

There are still (to this day)
  songs I cannot and will not
  listen to because
the ghost of the girl I once was
  lurks the chambers of my
Haunted House Heart
  and when I hear these particular songs
She slams doors
  rattles windows and will scream
until I remember
  She is still in there
    a Poltergeist forever.

Chicory not only was a few months away from having her degree, she found herself standing in the middle of a crossroads. One path led back to her past. The other kept her right where she was. The stress of it all was getting so heavy, she actually considered going to a physical crossroads nine nights in a row and wait for the Black Man himself to beg for answers. But that price would be too high, so she just continued to fret in silence.

"You're going to chew your fingers to the bone if you don't stop," Bea scolded Chicory as she gnawed on what was left of a fingernail. Bea had been not so subtly forwarding open teaching positions in the school she worked at. Chicory had begun her college path focused solely on fine art, but eventually added education. Chicory loved school. Her life had been changed by a teacher. She felt a calling to return the favor.

"Look," said Bea, "at some point you're going to have to throw it out to the universe and let the spirits guide you. Apply here. Apply back home. Apply in all fifty states and see who gets back to you first." Bea continued, "You know how I am about signs. There may not even be a position available in that county of yours. Have you even checked?"

Chicory shook her head before opening her laptop to rip the band aid off and check. They were sitting together at Bea's kitchen island. Bea was right. There may not even be anything available, or if there was, it might not be something Chic was qualified for.

"Ohhhhh," was all Bea said as she read over Chicory's shoulder. The middle school art teacher must have retired, because there, on the available positions list, was not only an opening, but what could also be interpreted as big fat neon electric sign.

"The school may not consider me because I'll be a first-year teacher," Chicory replied softly. But they both knew that was probably not the case. Her contract would be a lot cheaper than someone with experience and tenure.

Chicory decided to apply later since deciding to procrastinate when Azure handed her a book to read to him. The thought of leaving the farm and everyone on it threatened to smother her. Didn't she want to go home? Was it even home anymore? Didn't she extract herself from the jumble of Xavier limbs just that very morning, for him to pull her back and whisper sleepily, "Don't go." She couldn't bring herself to make decisions that day. Instead, she sat in the living room of the main house and read books that rhymed and pretended everything would be okay.

Of course, the next sign was so damn big it couldn't be ignored.

"You got some mail today, Chic," Gus called out from where he was watering plants from a rain barrel.

Chicory waved to him before grabbing the pile of letters off their catch-all kitchen table. She thumbed through the stack on her way out. Junk, school stuff, a bank statement, and a letter from the law offices of somebody and somebody else. They'd been trying to reach her for some time. Her Granny had always been saving for rainy days, and it would seem she saved up almost seven years' worth of rainy days, and the tax account she'd left for the property (address disclosed) that belonged to Chicory was short the money needed to pay this year by a few hundred dollars. She could pay the remaining balance, however there had been a few inquiries for purchasing the property and they would need to speak to her as soon as possible to move forward. Chicory called that very moment.

Xavier had never seen the look on Chicory's face that she was wearing when he entered the cabin. She perched on the edge of her bed looking completely lost. She handed him the letter.

"So that's it?" he asked angrily. "You just gonna up and go?"

She shook her head, "I don't know," she answered softly.

He recoiled as if she hit him. "Were you planning on asking me to go too?" The look on her face said it all. Sharp pain lanced through his chest.

"Your dream is to go to the West coast." She tried to justify her actions. "I wouldn't ask you to change your dream."

He was good and pissed now. "I have been in your bed since the night you asked me over … isn't it obvious my dream has changed?!" he shouted. Xavier had never raised his voice at her. Chicory started to cry. "I love you," he blurted. He'd wanted to tell her a thousand times, but it had never left his lips.

Chicory outright sobbed. Xavier started to gather the things he'd left intermingled with hers; picking up the fragments of the life they had just begun to share. "I see," he said resignedly.

"I told you I didn't have a heart to give you. I told you my heart was in a Holler miles and miles away. I told you I was broken. This was always going to be a dead-end road … " Chicory was trying to remember that conversation herself. What they'd said that first night they'd crossed the line. The first night they'd become lovers. How could they not have seen this coming? Sure, it was a dead-end road, but they'd barreled down it anyway, hadn't they?

In the end Xavier made the decision for her. "I don't want you to wonder if you made the right choice, I don't want you to choose. I want to be the only option." His arms full of collected laundry, Chicory watched as Xavier walked out of her door for the last time.

It was hard to argue with Bea's philosophical musings when, after everything that had happened to Chicory, plans fell so easily into place. The last few weeks of spring she was so busy preparing to leave, it was easier to ignore the hollowed out feeling in her chest. She figured she wasn't as heartless as she once thought.

As much time as they'd spent together, Chicory thought she'd at least see Xavier to talk, but he found every way to avoid her imaginable. He also let the new tenant in the Erin's old cabin nurse his broken heart. Chicory reckoned it was for the best.

Chicory cried when she packed her car with the boxed belongings she had accumulated. To think she had moved here with one bag, but now her life filled the car's entire back seat. Chicory cried even more when she swept the last of the dust out of her cabin. Her little home, the setting of some big memories. Chicory rested her hand on the doorway as she paused on her way out. "Thank you," she whispered into the wood.

Chicory had been spending her nights on the couch in the main house, she couldn't stomach sleeping in her bed alone. Besides, she could hardly sleep anyways, panicking over leaving her friends.

Azure had fallen asleep on Chicory's side, trapping her arm under his small body. Her arm was full of pins and needles but she didn't dare move him, she was soaking up every moment left. So of course she started to cry again.

Gus came over and kneeled down so he was eye level. "Chicory, this isn't going to be like last time. Last time you didn't have a choice. You're an adult now. If nothing is how you planned, just leave. It's that simple." He waited for her to nod her head in agreement before continuing. "My blood family weren't the best people. I was an orphan like you in some ways. But I found my true family. The family of my heart. You, Chicory, are a part of that … my Heart Sister. This isn't goodbye forever." He reached into his back pocket and pulled out his phone. "And we have these. I know you hardly use yours, but we can talk every day if you want. And despite everything you've taught me, I'm sure I'll always be asking questions about plants." They both smiled.

When it really came down to it, Chicory would be leaving with pieces of them that she'd carry with her always. She would never have eaten tofu without Bea. Or painted her fingernails black. She definitely wouldn't have gotten a tattoo or five, like Gus. Or know that if someone you love has a baby, you instantly love it as well. Chicory would always keep her door open for strays, taking them in just like Bea and Gus had done for her.

She'd carry pieces of Xavier with her too. She'd never know she could love a hip hop song as much as a folksy one. She'd never be able to pick up a comic without thinking of him. And she'd never have known what her body was capable of, she'd never know how she could show love with it, if he hadn't shown it to her first.

Gran had always said, "We were meant to meet the people that come into our lives. Whether it's a long time or a moment, good or bad, they shape us either way." Maybe Chicory was housed with the mean roommate to remind her she was strong. Maybe Chicory met Harleigh because that little girl needed a light in the darkness and Chicory could provide one. And maybe Chicory came to the farm because there were so many types of love and family, and she was in desperate need of both. For whatever the reasons, Chicory was the person she was today because of all of them.

In the dawn's soft glow, Chicory saw Xavier leaning on the hood of her car, his superhero shirt and cropped hair disheveled, like he'd rolled out of bed to wait for her. "Would you have left without saying goodbye?" he asked.

Setting down the bag of "road snacks" Gus had packed her, Chicory answered. "I didn't know if you'd want to see me."

He nodded, then looked away. He hadn't seen her in weeks and the sight of her was too much. Though he couldn't help himself as he found her eyes again.

"I was going to leave this on your step." She held out the gift she made him.

"Ahhh ... you planned to curse me, Chic?" he asked, only half joking.

"The opposite, actually," she laughed, before explaining. "A skeleton key so you'll never have anything blocking your way. An iron nail to protect you against anyone or anything that would do you harm. And a silver dime with a hole in it for good fortune and good luck. I tied them all together with a red string because I do love you Xavier in my own way. But you're right ... it's not enough. You deserve it all."

He took the talisman from her fingers and tucked it away in his pocket. He pulled Chicory into his arms, then sighed. "I let my pride get the best of me. I'm sorry I wasted the last of our time together. That's all I regret, Chic, nothing else." He spoke the words into her hair.

Chicory ran her hands up the column of his neck, to his jaw, and finally cupped his cheek. Their lips met in one last goodbye.

Xavier watched her car disappear before taking out the charm she'd made him. Unshed tears watered in his eyes. He didn't really cry much, he'd done a lifetime of crying when he was young. Xavier didn't know it yet, but he would have all of the things Chicory blessed him with and more. He would even eventually head West like he wanted ... but he would never see Chicory again.

It felt like eternity, but after mile after mile of pavement, there they were. The mountains, sprawled sensuously across the horizon like a long-lost lover. Their softened curves, dips and crevices so familiar ... yet not. So close.

PART THREE

CHAPTER 21
LORD WILLING AND THE CREEK DON'T RISE

Chicory had driven the almost five hours with only one stop, a greasy fast-food biscuit joint her Gran had taken her to a few times back when. The lawyer's office was in Downtown, which had always been a polished gem in the rough rock, with potted flowers and flags and even murals on the brick buildings. Chicory couldn't help feeling a bit of déjà vu. Though previously acquainted with the area, it seemed like a different place entirely. Like finding an old sweater that still fit but was snug in a way it hadn't been before.

Signing papers only took a few moments of time, and before she knew it, Chicory found herself standing at the door to the County Middle School. Surely this building was bigger last time she was here. It didn't look like they'd made any renovations, though there were trailers added to the back for extra classroom space, and an intercom preceded the always locked door. Someone on summer staff buzzed her in.

The former Guidance Counselor was now the Principal, he recognized Chicory's name, and it may have had some sway in his hiring her. The contract was cut and dry, and she'd sign it no matter what pay was offered to get her foot in the door. Chicory wanted to ask about her old friends, but what were the odds this man remembered them anyways. As their meeting was wrapping up he said, "I asked Mrs. Green our librarian to come in today and give you a little welcome and tour." There was a knowing smile about his lips.

"Why Chicory Goodwin ... Ain't you a sight for sore eyes?" said a voice from behind.

Silky auburn hair cascaded in a wave over the speaker's shoulders. The modest sundress she wore couldn't hide the hourglass shape of her curves. There was only one person Chicory had ever met with eyes the same shade as the bluebells that grow by the river in spring, Etta.

The sound that left Chicory was a whimper, a sigh and a laugh combined as she launched herself at her beloved friend without a care to what her new boss might think. As the reunited friends held each other, laughing and crying together, Mr. Lee dismissed the two of them with an "I'll leave you to it then" and a wave of his hand.

"Come on," Etta tugged Chicory out the office. "You don't need a tour, but we need to catch up."

Something Mr. Lee had said finally registered in Chicory's mind. "Wait ... Mrs. Green?—Em?—You and Em?"

Etta held up her left hand, showing off the glittering jewelry there. "Yes ma'am. We just did the courthouse. You were gone, Momma's gone now, so I couldn't bring myself to have any kind of fuss. Besides, we'd been living together—already it was a technicality."

Chicory stopped walking. "Your Momma passed? I'm so sorry, Etta," she said sadly. "What about your brothers? How are they?"

"It's alright. Momma's in a better place. She's certainly not suffering anymore ... Cash is stationed in Texas at boot camp if you can believe it. Sends us texts every day to tell us the temperature. Nelson is a senior this year and wants to do park service like Em."

Chicory couldn't help but interrupt. "Emory is a Park Ranger?" At Etta's "Yes Ma'am" Chicory laughed. "Of course he is, and you're a librarian ... Etta, it's perfect."

Etta's cheeks got rosy as she beamed, "Yeah, it's pretty great ... "

"What about Travis and Tucker?" Chicory asked about the youngest two boys.

"They stay with Em's parents during the week. Been that way since Momma's passing. Remember how they loved watching the cows through the fence when they were wee things?" Chicory smiled at the memory. "Well now they're little farmers. Emory Sr. has got them doing it all and they're happier than pigs in shit." Both girls giggled. She missed how people talked in these parts.

"What about ...   do you still see ...   " Chicory began awkwardly.

Thankfully Etta just knew and put Chicory out of her misery. "Hawk is around. He's still two shades from feral, we can snag him from time to time for dinner. He's shacked up with a gal in town, I reckon they're together, but you can never be sure with him."

Chicory stayed quiet. She didn't know exactly what she expected. Maybe nothing. Maybe more.

Etta broke Chicory's melancholic musings. "Where are you staying?"

"My old house. I haven't even been there yet," Chicory admitted.

"It's been closed a long time. If it's not fit to stay in, you come stay with us, alright?" They put their numbers in each other's phones with promises to see each other later. "Em's chomping at the bit to see you, too. Don't be a stranger. We gotta make up for lost time."

Etta watched as Chicory took in the surroundings and wondered what she'd been through and how had she found her way back after all this time. Boy, was she happy to see her, though. Truth be told, Chic looked a little peaked at the moment. Where were Etta's manners? "Did'ja eat?"

CHAPTER 22
DON'T COUNT YOUR CHICKENS BEFORE THEY HATCH

Being back in town was ... strange. Everything she vaguely remembered, but also didn't. New traffic patterns and shopping centers had been built to accommodate the area's growth, springing up in places where there once had been nothing but corn fields.

Chicory's compact car struggled to get up the sinuous Dark Holler, the car's engine and tires, small as they were, built for town, not country. First, she passed Widow Mary's fairytale cottage. She didn't expect the ancient woman to be alive, but the discarded bikes and strewn toys over the front yard confirmed she'd moved on. Chic wondered whatever happened to the old woman's cats.

Beholding the house she was raised in, Chicory's first impression was that time had been cruel to her childhood home. Free from human interference, Mother Nature had slithered her tendrils out to reclaim this piece of herself back. Waist high brown grass crept up to the sidewalk, the cracked concrete barely keeping it at bay. Moss grew thickly on the shaded side of the house while orange flowered trumpet vine climbed up the sunny one. Seeds had landed and taken root wherever the breezes had carried them. A helicopter had whirled and twirled, before sprouting in the corner of the gutter, now a maple sapling weighed it down. Termites had eaten away at the wooden shingles, and woodpecker holes were in the zigzag paths the birds made when trying to find the termites.

Wasp nests (thankfully) mostly vacant, covered the ceiling of the front porch. A few buzzing stragglers investigated the stranger in their midst. After unlocking the front door, sky blue paint chipping away, Chicory used her entire body to thrust open the humidity swollen wood.

The stagnant air assaulted her. Her eyes and nose watered at the offensive smell. There were new occupants living there now ... rodents, whose circular holes and scratches marred the walls, and who had tunneled through the couch, its stuffing fluff billowing from tears in the upholstery. The stench of their piss and droppings and the sweet rot of decay were too much for Chicory, and she couldn't stay inside any longer.

Gagging, she retreated back to the front porch. Succumbing to the crushing realization the house was uninhabitable, she collapsed on the porch step, burying her head in her knees. Though the sun was shining, rain drops pitter pattered around her. The devil was beating his wife. It was too much. She knew this feeling all too well. Despite her planning, here she was, a stray, once again.

Just then, Gus' words floated through Chicory's mind. She was grown now. She could figure it out. But first she needed a minute to sit there on the porch and feel sorry for herself.

Chicory may have sat there for two hours or two minutes, she wasn't entirely sure, before a soft, concerned voice interrupted her gloom.

"Excuse me ... Miss. Do you need help? This is private property." The mismatched eyes that looked up at him elicited a gasp. The daughter of his heart had finally returned.

There are more syllables in the Cherokee tongue for daughter than our own, and even though Chicory hadn't heard the language in such a long time, she instantly recognized it along with its speaker ... Winter, wearing a shirt covered in buffaloes and layered with beaded jewelry. More lines creased his face, but there wasn't a single gray in his jet-black hair. She noted the small details before being enveloped in a sweet-grass scented embrace.

"You're not staying in there tonight are you?" Winter asked, horrified at the thought.

"Not until the four-legged squatters get evicted," Chicory sighed.

"Come over to the house, then," he said over his shoulder to where Chicory already followed him, and they went over to the Winter's house together.

Seated at a round wooden table while nibbling on a tomato sandwich, Chicory's eyes followed Winter as he moved around the house. For the first time since she'd stepped back into her past, not much had changed. The walls were still wood paneling and the smoky scent of the wood stove clung to it all, even though it hadn't been used since spring. Knickknacks from the natural world were here and there. A weathered animal skull, a woven blanket, a hand painted peace pipe, a black bear pelt. After assuring him she didn't need anything else, Winter called a friend about the pest removal, but the man wouldn't be able to make it out until the next day. Once the critters were dealt with, she could get in there and clean. Chicory was never one to shy away from hard work, she was certain she could fix it up. Now she watched Winter text, bifocals perched on his long nose, slowly tapping out one letter at a time. Between the grim set of his mouth and his deflection, it was clear his son would not be joining them.

After spending a few hours with Winter, Chicory made her way back to town, taking up Etta's invitation to stay with them while she worked out secure lodgings. Turned out Winter had been dating a woman who owned a Holistic Spa downtown with a furnished apartment above it that she used as an Airbnb. Chicory could rent it month to month while she renovated the cabin. It never ceased to amaze Chic how the universe provided when you needed it most. Well, that, and a little help from friends.

GPS guided Chicory the few blocks away from the cute downtown area. After the disappointment with the state of her own house, pulling up to the three story brick Victorian brought a genuine smile to her face. Etta had her dream home!

Chicory had barely gotten the picket gate closed when a chorus of howls that were uniquely hound dog announced her arrival. She was a few steps up the wrap around porch, when the door opened to a smirking Emory Green.

"Well look what the cat drug in," he laughed, before scooping her up in a bear hug. Fitting, since Chicory thought he was the size of a bear too. After setting her down, Emory leaned in the doorway. The last rays of sun illuminated his golden hair. He still had his 'boy next door' good looks and his love of the weird as his 'I believe' UFO tee shirt suggested.

"Good to see some things haven't changed then," Chicory said, and Emory chuckled at that. Chic got down on her knees to greet the dogs that had been circling the two of them. Four beagles were patiently waiting for her to pet them, of course Emory taught them manners. The dogs fell over each other to get the closest. One of the pack had a gray muzzle and moved a bit slower than the others. "This can't be … "

"Oh yeah, my little Fern is still with me. I guess she's about twelve … maybe thirteen." He bent down to scruff under the dog's chin. Fern lovingly gazed back at him. That was the final straw that broke Chicory after this long, emotional day, and she sobbed into the little dog's fur.

At that moment, Etta arrived in swirl of auburn hair and flower covered cotton, just having finished setting up a room. She knelt herself alongside her beaten-down friend. "All right we gotcha now, girl." Etta gathered Chicory in her arms, still wanting to take care of everyone. They got Chic in bed. Despite being in a strange place she fell into a deep sleep, just needing to end that day, and try again tomorrow.

"Do you think she'll be alright?" Etta voiced her worry into Emory's broad chest.

He stroked her hair before answering. "Of course. She's got you looking after her now. She'll be right as rain," he answered honestly, and continued to offer his own comfort by holding Etta long into the night.

As Chicory began to wake up, the stress of the previous day came rushing back, but the smells of breakfast and coffee roused her from her head and the incredibly comfortable bed. Etta and Emory's home was immaculately clean and styled in chic vintage. Wallpaper, framed art, bohemian rugs and potted plants were masterfully woven into the décor. It was the most beautiful home Chicory had ever been in.

Chicory found her old friends in the kitchen which was about the size of her cabin back at Serendipity. "Good morning. This is quite the home you've made for yourselves. Y'all really know how to deck a place out," she said, before sitting down at the butcher block island.

Blushing, Etta replied, "when you've been dreaming of your own place for forever you can't help but go all out."

Emory added, "it was kind of a mess when we got it, which is how we got it ... as is. We did most of the work ourselves, so we can help you with Gran's. Plus whatever Etta wants I'll make sure she gets. Speaking of ... off to work I go." He kissed Etta, Chicory shyly turned away, not used to their affection but oh how it made so much sense.

"That suits you," Chicory said, nodding at his uniform.

"After my wife and my dog, my other love is the forest. Good luck today, Chic. Stay as long you need. It's good to have you back. And let me know when you're ready to go hiking," Emory added before grabbing his lunch and taking his leave.

"I'm not sure I've gotten over the last time he took us hiking," Chicory said to Etta sarcastically after Emory left.

"Ain't that the truth," Etta agreed. "Let's eat and then we'll tackle the day together." Etta put a plate and coffee filled mug in front of Chicory. Strengthened by her friend's encouraging words and offered vittles, Chicory did just that.

Pest control not only noticed the critters had moved into the cabin, but a few human footprints had been seen around the empty dwelling as well. He chalked it up to squatters, but Chicory thought it was awful strange they were barefoot. A tingling at the back of her neck made her uneasy and the prints just didn't sit right with her.

Chicory didn't come empty handed, but the pest removal cost hurt, badly, as did the security deposit on the apartment she was now renting. The huge dent in her savings was just another reminder that nothing was going as planned. However, the apartment was adorable, and she was used to living in a place half the size. It was also only two blocks away from the hubbub of downtown, which meant it was a short walk to the bookstore and coffee shop and the part time job she'd just taken for the time being. School was still a few weeks out and she could use the extra money while she was getting back on her feet.

Chicory kept busy. She waited tables at a trendy restaurant catering to out-of-towners that blessedly tipped well. On her days off she and Etta went thrifting for housewares. Other days were spent scrubbing out Gran's house while donned in respirators and rubber gloves. The days slipped by with a new kind of familiarity. The girls fell back into their easy friendship despite having changed in some ways. But in the ways that mattered, they stayed the same.

At the restaurant, the lingering glances the bartender gave Chicory reminded her she could seek out company—since despite it all she was lonely. She had FaceTimed Bea and Gus every other day since arriving, and they threatened to come get her at least a dozen times. But she was lonely for one person's company most ... and he had yet to see her.

CHAPTER 23
OUT OF THE FRYING PAN AND INTO THE FIRE

Hawk begrudgingly made his way up the curving Dark Holler Lane—which he'd incidentally been avoiding like the plague. But he needed a longer pole saw and his dad had one, and that bastard thought he was being sneaky by making his son come and get it. Between his dad, Etta and Em, Hawk was getting message after message, asking him why he had not seen Chicory yet. It was getting on his nerves. What did they think that he was going to do, just drop everything and run over there like some lovesick puppy? Hell no. He'd go when he was good and ready and at this point, he was staying away purely out of spite.

Never mind, he was barely sleeping, as restless as this whole bit was making him. He was worrying himself sick over the idea he'd run into her in town. He hadn't been able to relax. Every wisp of blonde hair he saw could be her. The memory of her face was so blurry he could have passed her already. Hawk was naturally ornery to begin with, but damn if he hadn't been worse than ornery.

With every inch closer to Gran's old house, his heart beat faster. Hawk's hands poured sweat as they white knuckled the steering wheel. Jesus Christ, was that a Prius? He crept by the lime green compact car that would be practically useless come cold weather. Not that he cared.

Just a hair past the property line Hawk couldn't help himself as he braked and pulled off to the side of the road, and sat there, needing a moment since he was hyperventilating. Fuck this. He just needed to see her in person so he'd stop making a mountain out of a molehill. He needed to see if she'd been worth holding this God damn candle for so long.

Sure he was a notch in more than a few bedposts, but if he was being honest with himself, he had never moved on. Most days he felt like garbage. Like someone had pissed in an empty neon green soda bottle and tossed it out their truck window. The bottle was now just rolling around the countryside. He was literal trash, and she was soft and lovely and perfect. Hell, did he really even know what she was anymore?

Jumping out of his seat with determination, he slammed the door loudly. He figured he'd just stop in and get it over with. Hawk made his way across the freshly cut grass, that mower looked awfully familiar, toward the front door of the cabin, but shit if she wasn't already standing there on the lawn waiting for him. Hawk's stomach dropped all the way to his feet when he had taken in the sight of her. Oh hell. She didn't look anything like his memories. No, this in the flesh Chicory was much, much worse.

Chicory had been rifling her way through the wooden chest that sat at the end of Gran's bed. Ghostly footsteps that paced the main room and birdsong were usually the only sounds that accompanied her most days, but today her ears picked up the sound of gravel crunching under tires. Not understanding how she knew, but she did. He'd finally come.

Chic watched Hawk war with himself in the truck's cab before she decided to go to him, and she'd only gotten as far as the front lawn, when he sprang out. He had not gotten much taller, just widened more. Energy pulsed from his stocky frame. Hawk looked so different since she'd seen him last, but she'd left a boy and came home to a man.

Tribal points were tattooed around his russet forearms. His skin was darker than she remembered, two tan lines indicative of sunglasses streaked both sides of his face. The bands of light color accentuated the laugh lines that would crinkle there when he was happy. But as Chicory watched the blood visibly draining from Hawk's face, it was pretty clear he wasn't exactly happy right now.

Hawk did not know how to feel. Relieved to see her looking so well. Angry. Sad. Even a little embarrassed. But Hawk was never good at handling a barrage of intense feelings all at once. He was completely overwhelmed. And when Hawk got overwhelmed, he detonated.

"What took you so long?" he accused.

"I could ask you the same," Chicory sharply replied. The comfort of its familiar rasp only fueled his fire.

"I thought you were fucking dead!" he hollered before stomping closer. His bare feet slapping hard on the grassy hill. "I waited for you for years and you didn't come ... so I thought you died."

Did he really?

Chicory rushed to explain, "I was grief sick for a while ... then I had a lot to figure to out. I had no money, no car, I was stuck, and had no way to get back here."

That made a lot of sense but Hawk was too worked up to stop. "Seven years ... how hard did you try? You look real good.

It must not have been that bad," he word vomited. Hawk knew he was being unfair, but he couldn't stop.

Chicory laughed but there was no humor in it. "Oh it was bad ... but I found my place. And I left what I'd carved out for myself there at the chance that I'd come back and you'd be here. How's that for truth? I left for just a snowball's chance in hell that maybe you'd still be here." Exhausted all at once, Chicory slumped onto the ground. She held up her arms in a shrugging gesture, giving Hawk a full view of the crescent moon scars that shone just enough to notice, and the tattoo inked on her inner arm. The image was a hawk feather and a chicory flower tied together with a ribbon. A red ribbon. Red for love.

The pressure in his chest was almost too much. Hawk walked up the rest of the grassy hill and dropped to his knees before her. "I'm so sorry, Chic." For yelling, for being mad, for not waiting, for being himself, for being an asshole.

"I'm sorry too," Chic admitted.

When they finally embraced none of it even mattered anymore.

Hawk flopped down in the grass next to Chicory, keeping their fingers interlocked between them. Just a soft tug on their clasped hands, and she lay down alongside him.

"Okay, tell me everything. Don't leave anything out," Hawk demanded.

Chicory talked until her voice was hoarse, until the fireflies came out and flitted around them like fallen stars and the last of the weight on her shoulders fell away with the day.

CHAPTER 24
POT CALLING THE KETTLE BLACK

Emory hiked along the almost overgrown trail as he happily responded to a nonemergency call. He enjoyed this perk of his job. Wildflowers added their pops of color in a sea of bright green growth. Summer bugs buzzed, but did not penetrate the protective layer of his strong deep woods repellent. His pack bounced with every purposeful step as he strode along, negotiating ground obstacles.

Two campers had reported something big and black tearing apart their site, which they had evacuated, not having followed proper food storing habits, nor had they acquired a back country permit to camp there in the first place. Most likely, Emory would just be picking up after them. "Leave-no-trace-behind *my ass*."

Emory still preferred trees to people (his glorious wife the exception), though no one would ever know it, since Emory was such a nice guy. It was hard to continue being nice, though, the world in the state it was in and all. But the way he saw it, the world was full of assholes and it needed all the nice guys it could get.

As he rounded the approximate area of the disheveled site, snorts and huffs preceded the creature. Not wanting to surprise the most likely suspect, a black bear, Em started to make a bunch of noise. The thing that pulled its face out of a chip bag to look up at him was big and black and fuzzy, and not what he expected.

Emory came to a halt. He never got scared exactly when he came across a creature. But there was always an unknown with a new acquaintance. Its large red eyes regarded him almost sheepishly as it licked the snack's grease from its elongated fingers.

"Quite a mess you got here," Emory said softly, and pointedly looked around at the destroyed pack and snack trash that littered the area. He hoped the smorgasbord would be worth the tummy ache this thing was going to have.

Not threatened by the hairless pink thing's presence by any means, the creature looked around for any remaining scraps, left the granola bars (they tasted like tree bark), grabbed the chocolate candy, and stood. It scratched its behind and stretched, making itself even taller than it already was. Towering over the hairless thing, it retreated a step. Unsure what it had to be afraid of, its kind didn't eat meat and that thing was too ugly to eat, anyways. Stomach rumbles were the only warning given before it passed gas. The ugly small creature gagged.

The cryptid lumbered away on hairy legs as long as Emory himself. What he hoped was mud, dry and crusted in the fur of its thighs, smelled otherwise. He watched it disappear into the trees, completely giddy to see it had wings. Emory wasn't even mad he had to clean up its mess, but he regrettably didn't get a good look at its feet.

Etta was chopping vegetables when Emory bounded in the front door, excitedly recounting his day. And he wondered why she never wanted to hike with him. She continued to prep dinner as he talked. Hawk and Chicory would be there in a few hours. It would be the first time all four had been together since Hawk finally stopped throwing his temper tantrums. Etta offhandedly wondered how it would feel, before telling her husband he probably didn't smell too far off from what he'd been describing for the last twenty minutes. Emory made his way to the shower; her point taken.

Chicory listened to the stories of her friends' last years of high school, it was a small sadness to have missed out, but mostly, she was happy they had each other.

Hawk watched her like a ... well ... a hawk. He couldn't help himself. She moved with a confidence she'd never had before. She talked with her hands; the nails painted black. Ink peeked out of her loose clothes, he wanted to see the designs so badly, but it wasn't any of his business, was it? And that strip of skin on her stomach that showed because her shirt wasn't quite long enough, was driving him to madness. The golden hoops in her ears and the one in her nose twinkled in the soft light. He listened as she talked about museums and art in that God's damn voice of hers and that feeling of being stupid crept along his neck. He became heated. They continued to talk about college and books and all sorts of shit he was too fucking stupid to understand. Or maybe he couldn't pay attention because it was boring, and he was an asshole with an incredibly short attention span.

"I gotta go." Hawk's chair scraped loudly on the hard wooden floors he had helped Emory refinish. He hoped he didn't scuff them. He barely registered their confused looks as he got the hell out of there before he had a full-on panic attack.

After Hawk's awkward departure, Chicory helped her friends clean up, ignoring the looks of worry they shared with each other. She thanked them for a lovely night before walking the short blocks to her apartment. She didn't want them to see her tears of disappointment. Just a few drops from each eye. Enough to make her eyes and nose red but not enough to warrant a tissue. She and Hawk were ... trying to find a place where he wasn't mad, and it wasn't weird, and they just hadn't found it yet. And as hard a pill as it was to swallow, Chicory had to admit to herself that maybe they never would.

"Hey, how was the trip down memory lane?" Beth asked Hawk as he came through the door. She was sprawled on the couch, watching a movie. He grunted in response and went into the kitchen.

She found him sitting at the dinette with an untouched longneck, staring off into space. Absentmindedly, he swiped his finger through the condensation on the bottle's side. She'd been too busy raising a two-year-old to notice the dark circles under his eyes. She'd been meaning to talk to him, but they'd been passing ships lately. Sighing, she began, "Hawk, you know I care about you, but if Evan walked through that door, I'd put your ass out of it." Hawk looked at her then. She continued, "But Evan is dead, and I won't get the second chance you're getting."

"I don't deserve a second chance," he whispered.

"You deserve a hell of a lot more than you give yourself credit for. If you hadn't moved in here after Evan died I would have lost the house. I don't know if I could've taken care of my son. Cleaned my house. Fed myself. Hawk, you're a great friend. I'd be lying if I said sharing your bed wasn't a perk also." They shared a smile.

And now, the thing she'd been waiting to tell him. "My parents asked me to move back to Florida. They've been asking actually. I've been putting it off, but I think it's best. Too many ghosts here."

"What about EJ?" he asked. EJ isn't his baby, but Hawk had a hand in raising him in the last year.

"I think we should cut ties while he's young. I'm already going to have explain his daddy is in Heaven and he'll only know him through stories and pictures. I don't want to confuse him by telling him about someone else too." That was the real truth that had been weighing on her mind. The real issue she'd been putting off. She felt a little bad for leaning on him the way she did and yet wanting to end things between them. The unexpected arrival of his long lost first love was perfect timing. It was the last push she needed to follow through. She didn't want to hurt Hawk, but her son would always come first.

He had been quiet while she talked, he'd be sad to see them go but also agreed. "Okay. What's next then?"

"I have one last favor ... Help me pack?"

Emory finished loading the dishwasher before turning to his wife who was still worrying herself over whatever was going on with Chicory and Hawk. He wanted a happy ending as much as she did, but well, life didn't always work that way. She was going to make herself bleed if she didn't stop chewing her bottom lip anxiously. What she needed was a distraction and luckily Emory knew just the trick.

"Loretta?" he asked through a smirk as he dried his large hands on a dish towel.

"Yes, husband?" she answered back sarcastically. There are only a handful of situations where he said her full name and she shivered with anticipation.

"You must have misplaced one of your books on my nightstand?" He raised an eyebrow.

"Oh my ... which one?" She knew exactly which one.

"Something with a shirtless man on the front. I couldn't help but open to where you'd bookmarked ... page 127. How many times did you read page 127, Loretta?" With each word he crept closer and closer. "Hmmmm?"

"Once or twice," she lied again. She probably read it a hundred times. Etta squeals as he throws her over his shoulder and carries her upstairs to where he showed her he had read page 127 a few times himself.

CHAPTER 25
SHIT OR GET OFF THE POT

Hawk's pickup wasn't the best on gas but it had four-wheel drive. He was gonna need it to get up and down Dark Holler Lane since he was moving back into his childhood home. A few cardboard boxes, a trash bag full of clothes and the truck he'd been driving were all he had to his name. Ain't that depressing.

As he made his way around the bend, Granny's house came into view. He was hoping to avoid Chicory but there she was, standing out front and talking to someone. What the fuck was Tommy doing there? Hawk's vision went red in the way that Tommy had always had a way of instigating trouble. Moving forgotten, he pulled in behind Chicory's car.

Her hair was in a bun on top of her head in a style he'd never seen her wear before. Her graceful neck was on full display and it tripped him up. "What's up?" he asked, out of breath.

"Not good news actually," Chicory replied without missing a beat. "Tommy is here to inspect the house," she added, her hand shielding her eyes from the sun as she looked out over the property. Tommy was in a shirt with his company's logo embroidered on the breast, his uniform and a glance to the work truck in the grass, confirmed he was there on business. Hawk relaxed a bit.

"Yeah ... Our Chicory has quite a bit to think about," Tommy's eyes glistened as he tried to rile Hawk. "Here's my card. Call me if there's anything you need." It was not Hawk's overactive imagination; Tommy definitely emphasized the word 'anything.' Maybe Tommy wouldn't be such a prick if Hawk wasn't so easy to bully.

Chicory raised an eyebrow as the two oversized boys provoked each other. "I gotta get out of this sun," she stated before heading to the house's shaded front step.

Once she was out of earshot, Hawk blurted, "what was that about? You called her ugly once, remember?"

Tommy clapped Hawk on the shoulder and laughed. "Bro', I lied." He held up his arms in surrender. "I've always had the hots for her."

"I thought that was Etta," Hawk yelled at Tommy's retreating back.

"Her too!" He turned around and gave Hawk a saucy wink and blew him a kiss.

Fuming, Hawk squeezed down next to Chicory on the step, their legs flush. He'd give her more space but there wasn't any, plus it was an excuse to touch her. Sorry, no more room.

"What was that back there?" Chicory asked. Despite getting out of the sun her cheeks and shoulders are already streaked with pink.

"Oh we have a love hate relationship," he answered.

"What does that even mean?" Chicory shook her head, the movement caused her body to rub against Hawk's. They both pretended not to notice.

"I hate him ... but I also understand him. He's consistent. So I also kind of love him. It's sick. We've probably been in like fifteen fist fights," he laughed. Chicory looked like she was going to ask more so Hawk beat her to it with his own question. "Okay, so what was the bad news?"

"He said between the foundation, the water damage, the pest damage, and the roof, he doesn't think it's worth fixing. But, he said we have plenty of room to build a new house and he can use parts of this one in it like the sink and the wood stove. Thankfully the table survived," Chicory sighed. Building a whole new house sounded ... expensive. And likely not happening any time soon.

"That's not too bad," Hawk said, like he knew what they were even talking about anymore, he could hardly concentrate with her so close. Her smell invaded his senses.

"What is all that?" She gestured to the stuff in his truck.

He flinched. "Oh ... yeah, I'm moving back home."

Surprised, Chic asked, "What happened with ... Beth was her name, right?"

"She's moving back to Florida to be with her family." He had finished helping load the U-Haul that morning, watched her drive away into the sunset and realized he was completely okay.

He could feel Chicory's eyes on his face as strongly as if she was touching him. "Are you okay?" she asked while searching his face for a reaction.

He looked her directly in the eyes, one green, one green and brown. "Yes." The finality of the that one word closed off further discussion. Black ink peaked out of the shirt Hawk was wearing, it caught Chicory's attention. He'd thrown on the button up hastily and left the top more open than he would've if he'd known he'd be seeing Chic.

"May I?"

When he nodded, she pushed his shirt open further to reveal the tattoo covering his whole chest. A Hawk in flight spanning from collar bone to collar bone, chicory flowers clutched tightly in the bird's talons. The plant's roots spread down over his heart like veins. It was evident in the faded ink he'd had this tattoo for quite some time. Hawk trembled under the light tracing of her fingertips. They had moved so close together they could feel each other breathing. Emboldened, Chicory lifted her hand to the nape of Hawk's neck, to the hair that was curling there. The strands were still silken soft as she pinched them between her fingers. "How long have you been wearing it short?" He could feel her whispered words on his face.

"I cut it right after ... " he trailed off, not needing to elaborate. Taking her hand from his neck he pressed a kiss to her palm. Chicory's sharp intake of breath echoed in the heavy moment. "How many times have we sat on these steps? I have so many memories of us, but we're not us anymore, are we?" he asked almost shyly.

It was the question she'd been thinking about since he stormed out of dinner. "We'll always be us ... but we're part of nature too. We change. We grow ... maybe from here we can grow together ... "

The two friends regarded each other before meeting in the last bit of space between them. This touch of lips was not like their last kiss. The sloppy tear-soaked goodbye. This was a sensual dance. A slow perusal as they explored each other's mouths, getting reacquainted with their shapes. A second first kiss to start their second beginning.

Hawk and Chicory did what anyone else who was falling in love for the second time would do. They texted each other throughout the day when they weren't together. In between work (school was about to start) Chicory made lesson plans and supply lists she hoped there would be funding for, the two would meet for lunch or dinner. Chicory kept her part time job; she was saving to build a house now after all. Hawk would sometimes sit at the bar and order food, all the while giving stank faces to the bartender. After long days trimming trees and even longer nights saving lives, Hawk would fall asleep easily. Often on Chicory's futon. Especially if she played with his hair.

When Hawk saw Chicory in the fitted dress she was wearing that day, his first thought was how easy it would be to remove. She'd kept him hot and bothered for weeks, he thought this was the moment he would finally combust. His fire was instantly doused when she said, "Let's go to the swimming hole." Though if he was being honest, he was a little surprised she hadn't mentioned it sooner. "Alright," he concedes.

His dad had always kept the trails cleared and the trail to their old spot was no exception. Hand in hand, they made their way easily down the wooded path.

Dappled sunlight sparkled on the water's surface. Chicory smiled softly at Hawk before removing her dress, then stood before him in nothing but freckled skin. Hawk then knew why other women's beauty did not stir his soul like this; he'd already seen the most beautiful woman in the world. A thought came unbridled to him. The long ago dream of their multicolored children running wild in these very woods. "If you leave again, I won't survive," he admitted.

Chicory tugged his shirt over his head before replying. "Good thing I'll be here until I die, and you'll bury me right here in this very spot so I can give back to the land that gave so much to me. And if you're still standing six feet above, my ghost will be right next to you and every time you feel a soft breeze on your cheek, it'll be me reminding you I'm still here." They landed in a knot of entwined limbs, clambering to get so close, nothing between them. Chicory's knees land on either side of him, bones digging into the earth. The scent of Hawk's skin mingled with the heady perfume of mountain laurel in every panting breath.

Chicory was home. Not Dark Holler or the mountains of Appalachia. Not the apartment. Not the farm. No place Hawk was not ... but right here. He was home.

CHAPTER 26
WHAT GOES AROUND COMES AROUND

I don't mind melancholy.
I savor it like dark chocolate.
Bitter to some, decadent to others.
It thickens my blood. I move so slow.
I hear every whomp whomp of my heart.
I feel every eyelash.
Daffodils break free of their dirt tombs,
Yellow faces turned toward an equally yellow sun.
I didn't think I could or would,
Miss the Winter that never came.
And wonder if I'll ever feel the
    icy kiss of a snowflake again. And sigh.
We buzz like newly awoken insects
For Spring but it's such a time for doing.
Why don't we appreciate January more?
Long dark days where we rest
And catch up on last year's sleep.
Then we find ourselves sitting on the cusp of Summer.
Trying and failing to get one last sip of the season
                from our cupped hands.
But the sands of time are more liquid in mass
And the days drip through our fingers
No matter how hard we try to hold them.
And the seasons they change again and again.

Chicory could not sleep. The wind hollered something fierce, rain pounded at the windows. Hawk had gone out there in all that mess, it was an on-call night and he'd been called.

The house groaned under the weather's onslaught. Chicory's body groaned too. With each passing day her bones and organs moved, her skin stretched taught, all to accommodate the growing babe in her. Still weeks away from birth, Chicory couldn't imagine she'd get bigger, but just as her mother and her grandmother before her, she would.

Resigned to staying awake, Chicory shuffled to the kitchen and filled a kettle from Gran's old sink that now lived on in this new house. The house she and Hawk would raise their family in, that sat on the land they themselves grew up on. It took years to build, but what's a few years when you've got forever?

Her reflection stared back at her from the dark window as she looked outside, hoping all the animals living on their backyard farm were hunkered down and the rain didn't beat down the garden that still grew despite the chill in the air.

In the flash of lightning brightness, Chicory saw a tree had come down on the goat fence. The last thing she needed tonight was chasing wandering goats over the mountainside. Besides, the doe had two little ones. If they got out, they'd be easy pickings. Chicory had best check it out.

In the back of the house Chicory had a mud room put in, an outerwear catch all. She shoved her swollen feet into her muck boots. Her coat didn't fit anymore so she wrapped one of Hawk's around her rounded frame. Just before she stepped into the night, she got a feeling. There was a gun rack on the wall for easy access. They'd had to shoot at more than a few unwelcome guests looking for a chicken dinner. Something told her to take the rifle with her, that prickling feeling that something ain't right.

She made her way slowly on the slippery path to the barn. She was almost there when she heard the screaming.

It took Chicory's mind a moment to catch up to what her eyes were seeing. The two young goats were bleating in terror, trying to get as far away from what was leaning over their mother, Buttercup. That was the little goat's name because she had golden fur and eyes. Those eyes were open and vacant as a white form curled over the rest of the animal. Sickening slurping sounds were loud enough to be heard over the panicked bleats. The thing making the sounds looked up from where it feasted on entrails—The Moon Girl.

Chicory gasped. She saw blood running in rivulets down its chin, making bright red trails on its pale skin, all the way past its saggy breasts. The creature stood and stepped over the mutilated carcass. Scar tissue patterned the side of its face where all those years ago Chicory had slammed a rock into it. The eye there, once black, now filmed over. The Moon Girl's head tilted, regarding Chicory inhumanly, nostrils flaring to breath in her scent. Chicory was filled with molten terror as the creature, covered in goats' blood, grinned revealing dirty, pointed teeth, with flapping pieces of torn flesh caught between them.

Muscles tensed, but before the Moon Girl could attack, Chicory pulled the trigger. Her adrenaline was pumping too fast to aim better than a shoulder graze, which only made the creature angrier. Chicory tried to run as fast she could to what she hoped was safety—to her house—

The Moon Girl easily covered the distance between them. The sounds it made, the grinding stone on stone sound Chicory had hoped to forget, its ragged breathing getting closer and closer until it dove onto Chicory's legs. She only had a moment to turn herself to not land on her front, taking the impact on her hip. The pain that exploded through the bone was nothing compared to the sheer and utter agonizing fear Chicory felt as the creature moved up her legs. It was so similar to before, Chicory, frozen with fear, as this monster slithered over her body.

Lightning cut through the sky again. The flash caused the Moon Girl to hesitate, wincing, to cover its remaining sensitive eye. That pause was enough for Chicory to buck the creature off her. As it tried to climb back on her prone form, Chicory kicked at its face as hard as she could. The creature's screams accompanied the sound of crunching bone. Kick. Kick. And again. Chicory wasn't just fighting for her own life now; this thing would be delighted to rip her baby from her. The Moon Girl scuttled back, like a crab, to make her escape, but Chicory had decided this was the last time the two of them would ever meet again. Remembering the rifle still clutched in her grip, she aimed at the Moon Girl, and this time she didn't miss.

Tears streamed from Chicory's face, hot against her cheeks, stark contrast from the cold rain drops that still came streaming down. Chicory's heart raced as she managed to get to her feet to inspect the body. She used the barrel of the gun to flip it over, confirming there wouldn't be a next time.

Chicory was surprised to see red blood leaking from the bullet's hole, discomforted by the human-like color. She thought it would be blue or black. The Moon Girl's life drained into the storm puddles underneath its body. The unmarred side of its face looked young now, free of its hunger. What made a monster? Was this creature a monster for simply no other reason than being higher on the food chain? Was this a creature of times past, long before humans took over it all? Chic felt like the monster now. She never wanted to kill the Moon Girl ... but as she ran her hand over the swell in her middle, she understood the choice was already made and she'd do it again if she had to. This was Appalachia, and just like the people that first came to this wild land, she would do what she had to do, to survive. Just like her Gran taught her.

Did you see something?
No, you didn't.

An Epilogue

I couldn't help myself. I played with the child, showing quick glimpses.

The child, a boy, caught my attention with his odd eyes. One green as a new leaf, one brown as upturned earth. We play a peek-a-boo game. The young ones are always easier to trick. They love games.

I love to play games too.

Here in the shadows of the forest I can smell the sunshine on the child's freckled skin. So soft, that skin. So easy to open to get to the gooey bits underneath. I inhale deeply. This is as close to daylight I will get. Tasting it on my tongue I salivate.

"What are you doing?!" screeches another child. This one, a girlchild, just a little bigger than my prey. She grips the arm of the small boy, dragging it further away. "You know the rules. Mommy taught you."

"But I thought I saw a kid in there," the smaller child whines. "I heard it laughing."

"Even more reason to stay away." I heard the girl say as she fled, taking my meal with her.

Damn rules. I have rules too. I cannot follow them into the light. I must stay in the black between the trees.

Barely a moment passes before another figure comes to the edge. Just out of reach. This one has strange eyes too, but unlike the child, this one would never fall for my tricks. Even though the witch doesn't acknowledge my presence, she throws handfuls of herbs towards where I hide. I don't like that one bit. They smell wrong.

I move on silent feet, blending deeper into the woods, off to find an easier catch. Maybe I will head to the trails. Those flimsy shelters erected for sleep are no better at protecting my victim than their own pliable outer layer. One nail slid down is all it takes to split something open wide. I admire them, my long sharp nails. So good at tearing.

Hunger gnaws at my belly. Hunger is all I know. Deep, dark and old. My belly rumbles again. Nothing can protect whoever dares to venture out here tonight. No, tonight I *will* eat ...

GIVING CREDIT WHERE CREDIT'S DUE

I have a confession to make ... I am not native to Appalachia, nor do I currently reside there. My family and I live in the foothills of the Blue Ridge mountains and in the years we've lived here I have fallen more and more in love with the hills. While this particular work of fiction is vague in its location, it is directly inspired by some of my favorite Virginia and West Virginia towns.

This story has been inside my head for a while now, but as it was starting to take a physical shape, I was mourning the loss of a decade's old friendship. That loss hit me harder than any romantic teenage heartbreak ever did, and in dwelling on it, I realized those friendships that shape us early on never fully leave us. Since I began this book we've reconnected, I don't know exactly where it leaves us, but she's forever imprinted on my soul.

I've always been a fan of the "par-a-normal", but the first house Joe and I lived in when we moved to Virginia was haunted. It's one thing to say you believe, but to experience a haunting firsthand is another beast entirely. Since my brain had irrefutable evidence that ghosts exist, I can honestly say I've seen more and more. So much that I wholeheartedly believe that there is still mystery in the world, so much unexplained. Isn't that awesome?

I'm not saying that I believe the creatures on these pages are real, but I read something about Cryptids that really stood out to me ... it said, even if the creatures themselves don't exist, that doesn't mean the stories aren't real. I love that. And even though I have taken a lot of creative liberties in these pages, they are inspired by people's stories, close encounters and experiences.

I know I took a pretty hefty risk when I wrote about Momma Jo, but I wanted to include burn talking in this and that's how the story unfolded. Writing this book has been a healing journey for me, I'm not proud of this but I hold a grudge, and in my journey to forgive one of the things, I've realized parents make the choices they think are best because they are trying their best.

I enjoy reading stories with love sprinkled in so it's inevitable I write them that way as well. I don't think I would do it successfully if it wasn't for Joe. We live a charmed life for sure. Thank you for sharing it with me.

Beta readers are supposed to be folks you don't know, but it's hard to let your innermost thoughts out into the world so I ask those I trust to read them first.

Thanks to Shea for being the first to read this, as part forest pixie I needed her to make sure I was doing the woods justice and the reader felt lost in them at times. She also told me about her "daylights" and I thought it was the cutest.

Thanks to my Stepmonster Maci, believe me when I say, if it was bad, she'd tell me ... and not sugar coat it one bit. She not only kept notes while reading (I know how many times I wrote the word breast), but she also made me promise nothing would happen to Fern.

Thank you Jess for being mad at what I put these characters through. When someone talks to you about characters you've made up like they're real it gives an author the confidence they need to finish.

Frances, you should be an editor. You caught all my big mistakes and talked me though pieces I needed to figure out. Thank you for reading and reading deep.

Nothing I write would be brought to the hands of readers without Suzanne, she truly has made my dreams come true and I will forever be grateful.

When someone is stuck on Old Rag, the rescue helicopter flies over my house. Did you know search and rescue teams are made up of volunteers? I wanted to be sure I did the men and woman who make up emergency services justice by sounding like I knew what I was talking about, and so I wanted to say a special thank you to Lisa Davis who answered any and all questions I had about park rangers, search and rescue and firefighting.

Thanks to Kim for answering questions about teaching contracts for me. Bless your hearts teachers.

I want to take a moment to also thank my local indie bookstores. Thank you for everything you do to support local authors like me struggling to not feel like a fraud. Please visit The Open Book in Warrenton, Hundred Acre Books in Culpeper and Spelled Ink in Orange.

Appalachian culture is vast, big and beautiful like the mountains of the area. I hope I did it justice. I hope you read this book and felt my love for the area, my love for it's old ways and folk customs ... and yes, even my love for it's monsters.

Lastly thank *you* for reading these words.

About the Author

Jen Poteet is a creative thinker and doer dwelling on the edge of the Blue Ridge Mountains with her husband, Joe, their kids, and a menagerie of pets. When she isn't daydreaming or exploring, she can be found at Black Sheep Studios, the tattoo studio and art gallery she owns and operates with Joe. Her other books include *Secondhand Heart,* a quirky romcom for fellow weirdos and *A Night Under the Circus Tent,* an illustrated children's book.